IN A FLASH

Flash Fiction

By
Paula Parente

ACKNOWLEDGMENTS

Many thanks to my partner, Tim G Young, for his love and support. And also, especially to my sister, Samantha! And her husband, Richard Sayer (photojournalist), and my parents, Sam and Beverly - who all stick with me through thick and thin. Thanks also to Jared D'costa and the team at Amazon who helped make this book possible.

TABLE OF CONTENTNS

Part One

LIFE

Jessica kicked off her black loafers, heaved a heavy sigh, dropped her canvas knapsack into the chair by the door, locking it behind her. It had been a long, difficult evening shift, flipping hamburgers, shaking baskets of fries from the dripping hot oil, and serving customers by rote. Not to mention, her boss at the fast food restaurant had yelled at her - something about not ringing up the coupon properly. So hankering for a treat, Jessica stopped at the local convenience store and picked up a carton of mint chocolate chip ice cream, and as an afterthought, purchased a couple of lottery tickets. After changing out of her grease-spattered uniform into a comfortable pair of jeans and dark purple pullover sweater, and dipping her spoon several times into the cool, creamy confection, she reached into her coin jar for a nickel, sat down at the kitchen table covered with the sunflower and daisy vinyl tablecloth, and began to rub the squares on the first lottery ticket.

Living on the fourth floor in this tiny, cramped, though somewhat neatly-kept apartment on Broad Street, in the run-down section of the city, not to mention her debilitating job of five years, made Jessica long for something better. Maybe some lottery tickets were the way out. She rubbed harder at the squares, the grey bits, shreds of dust clouding over the small card. She pushed them away, revealing one matching number, then two ... four ... six matching numbers.... What? Was she seeing this correctly? Jessica squinted at the numbers, picked up her glasses to get a better look. It couldn't be ... but yes ... she had won! It was the grand prize: five hundred thousand dollars!

Jumping up and knocking over her hand-painted ruby metal chair, she danced around the kitchen, laughing, crying, shouting at the top of her lungs. Big dreams, like popcorn popping erupted in her mind's eye. First ... quit her job. Second ... travel! For a long time she had wanted to go places: tour the temples in Japan, visit Bermuda and swim with the dolphins, hike up to the ruins of Machu

Picchu in Peru, visit Paris, London, Venice - check off her bucket list. Words from Hunter S. Thompson, or at least as close as she could remember them, ran through her head: *Life should not be a journey to the grave with the intention of arriving safely in a pretty and well preserved body, but rather to skid in sideways in a cloud of smoke, thoroughly used up, totally worn out, and loudly proclaiming "Wow! What a ride!"*

Jessica let out another whoop, skidded over to the phone, ticket in hand, ready to call her sister, Rhonda, who lived with her son in an apartment a couple of blocks away. But her fervent emotion was interrupted by the phone itself, which had just begun to ring. Who could be calling at this late hour? It was after eleven thirty … though contacting her sister with this great news, Jessica felt, warranted a call.

She picked up the phone. It was Rhonda. "Jess! Can you come over now?" "What's wrong?"

"Brandon. He has a temperature of one hundred and four point two, and I left my car in the shop today. A transmission problem. I've got to take him to the ER. Can you drive us?"

"Sure. Of course. I'll be right over." Jessica ran to get her purse, threw on a light jacket, pulled her car keys off the charcoal-colored octopus hook, and realizing that early tomorrow

morning was trash pick-up, she grabbed the pile of junk mail, tossed it in with the rest of the garbage and rushed out of the apartment, dropping the bag in the can on the sidewalk.

At first her car had trouble starting. "Come on!" Jessica shouted, hitting the steering wheel. It turned over three times before the engine finally kicked in. She sped down the street, tires screeching as she rounded the corner. Leaving the motor running, Jessica beeped the horn in front of her sister's apartment building. Rhonda rushed down the stairs carrying Brandon, limp and weak in her

3

arms. At that hour, hardly a car was on the road and they made it to the ER within ten minutes. It didn't take long before Brandon was seen by a doctor, who immediately began treatment to lower his fever. The doctor told the sisters that he wanted to keep an eye on him, not wanting to release the boy until he was sure to be alright. For several hours Jessica and Rhonda sat with Brandon, took turns getting up for coffee or stretching their legs. At one point, while Brandon was sleeping, they looked at pictures and read stories from some of the *Better Homes and Gardens* magazines they found in the waiting room.

Finally, when Brandon's temperature had significantly lowered, the doctor said he could go.

The sun was coming up as the threesome drove home; Brandon was fine and the sisters were relieved, their spirits soaring. Everyone laughed and hugged goodbye. Brandon and Rhonda climbed the stairs back to their modest residence.

As Jessica drove the rest of the way home alone, her thoughts turned to the winning lottery ticket, her excitement, which had been dulled by the night's events, returning. She couldn't wait to cash it in and begin her new life.

Entering her apartment she headed straight for the end table housing the phone. The ticket wasn't there. She could have sworn she brought it over to the phone when she was about to call her sister. Maybe it was on the kitchen table. No, not there either. Jessica stopped, gathered her thoughts, retraced her steps. Then it hit her, like a whizzing baseball contacting her straight in the gut. In her frenzy and turmoil, she had dropped the ticket on top of the pile of junk mail, and not taking the time to look closely, she had grabbed the whole pile and tossed it in the garbage bag, ticket included; now it was outside in the trash can.

Jessica frantically dashed down the steps inside the apartment house and out the front door. Maybe the garbage man hadn't come yet, though it was already past seven am, his usual pickup time. Upon opening the can and seeing it empty, she let out a loud, heartsick shriek. Oh no!

Jessica let the refuse can cover drop with a clang, covering her face with her hands. Through a bee sting of swelling tears and short constricted breaths, her panic rose, peaked … and then she switched gears: Jessica was livid, furious, filled with a burning fire. This was NOT happening. THIS was not GOING to happen!

In that second, Jessica made a fist-clenching, passionate, calculated decision. She would go down to the city dump and pick through every single piece of trash if she had to. And she would not stop until she found that ticket! Jessica jumped in her car, started the engine, the words from Hunter S. Thompson ringing in her head: *Life should not be a journey to the grave …*

SHARON

The woman in the midnight blue dress with the big black dog arrived promptly at four pm.

Sharon, who answered my add, the one I placed in the local newspaper two nights before, looked unbelievably beautiful, and for a moment, I almost lost my nerve. Me, my name's Steven, and I was a guy thirty years old, never had a date, never had someone to love and love me back - all because of a deformity that covered the left side of my face. From birth, my skin was covered with a big, bubbled red blotch - and there was nothing I could do about it. And even if I could, neither my parents nor I had the money to pay for that kind of operation.

So I resorted to putting adds in the paper: dog-lover, looking for a friend to share long walks through the park, music and movies, possible romance.... Sometimes I got an answer, sometimes not. Even when I did manage to set something up, I'd get there, take one look at the girl and chicken out, not having the nerve to approach them. So many girls, I imagine, feeling hurt, wondering what the heck happened. But this girl, Sharon, who stood alone at the edge of the restaurant's courtyard, wearing the telltale yellow rose pinned to her dress, somehow seemed different. Perhaps it was her curly red hair, which reminded me of my favorite aunt when she was younger, or maybe it was her smile that seemed to brighten everything around her. Whatever the reason, this time I decided to take the chance.

I pushed back my chair, stood up from the table shaded by a very big umbrella, and gave a welcoming wave in her direction; when she saw me, her smile widened. Tightening the leash on her Labrador Retriever, this gorgeous girl began walking, weaving her way past the crowded tables of people eating, talking, laughing, and enjoying the unusually warm spring weather.

When she got within ten feet of me, she stopped; Sharon had seen my face. Her dog barked loudly, nervously. I expected her to turn around and leave. But she continued forward, moving slower, still smiling. She held out her hand when she reached me.

"Hi, I'm Sharon. Nice to meet you, Peter." I took her hand in mine, but not before noticing the bright discoloration, the big red bubbled birthmark branded on the back of her hand.

NO IDEAS

Donna sat at the beautifully designed, terra cotta tiled table, pen in hand, fresh out of ideas. She stared at the blank, white page, knowing the deadline for her article was looming fast. Of course she was grateful for her travel writing job she acquired three months ago, but she hadn't planned on the pressures that went along with it.

Now, here she was in Rome, at a small cafe at the edge of a quaint piazza, with life bustling all around her. Why couldn't she come up with the perfect idea? Yes, there were many writers before her who covered the subject of Rome, it's culture and it's people. So Donna was looking for something new, different, exciting - something that would grab her boss's attention and help her keep the job she worked so hard to get. She took a sip of camomile tea and a bite of her chocolate biscotti while scanning the scene. Couples were walking hand in hand, stopping to steal a kiss. Families sat along a wall housing a decorative fountain. And teenage boys were skateboarding nearby, the harsh sound of wheels to pavement jarred her ever so briefly.

Just then a stylish gentleman wearing a royal blue tie and black velveteen jacket quickly stepped up to her table and sat down nervously. "Here, take this," he whispered as he handed her a large, dark brown shopping bag. "Now come with me," the man said forcefully, grabbing for her arm.

Donna shook her arm loose and pointed to police who were patrolling the area not far away. "I'll scream," she hissed. The man, now visibly more anxious, jumped up and took off before Donna could make a sound and the cops could get a look at him.

Donna knew she could still be in danger; what if he came back, but ... as she opened the paper bag and peeked inside to see the beautiful oil painting of sunflowers signed by Van Gogh himself, well ... she knew she had the story of a lifetime.

BIG CITY

The big city groaned in the morning sun. It was just starting to come alive with the screeching of tires, roaring bus engines, beeping horns, taxi doors slamming, and people yelling above the clamor. Another day on the horizon, and Bob, one of millions, was on his way to work at the hugely successful advertising agency that boasted a large number of multi-million dollar, high- roller clients.

He stepped into the silver-chromed elevator and rode up to the fifty-seventh floor. The door beeped open; Bob exited and strode down the hall to his corner office overlooking Central Park. It wasn't five minutes later when his secretary, June, rushed in and started rattling off the list of appointments he had for the day; all the while Bob nervously chewed on his Cherry-Cheese danish and slurped his hot, Columbian Roast coffee.

"Cancel my ten o'clock," he barked, obviously perturbed. "Better yet, cancel my eleven and twelve too."

"But Mr. Epstein," she stammered, "your clients have …"

"No," he cut her off. "I need you to do this for me. Now!… And come to think of it, I'd also like you to call off the rest of my day."

"As you wish," his secretary shrugged and shuffled out of the office.

Bob sat quietly in his swivel chair, not sure what to do next. The only thing he was sure of was that he couldn't take one more day in that suffocating, soul-stealing, time-trapping office.

He jumped up and sped down the long hallway lined with tightly-packed, dull grey cubicles, passing by four co-workers who chased after scattered papers and reports that had fallen to the floor. He entered the elevator once more and hit the ground floor button. Once on the street, Bob squeezed and dodged through crowds, whereupon entering the park he collapsed on a newly painted brown wooden bench. Breathing a deep sigh of relief, followed by several shorter breaths just to calm himself, Bob stared at the ground, bewildered. After several minutes had gone by, he reached for the cell phone in the pocket of his light tan, linen suit jacket, and decided to check his email. Scanning down the long list, one title in particular caught his eye: "The Big City - Is it Time for a Change?"

"That's odd," Bob thought, as he had just been thinking the very same thing. He clicked to open. Just then a flash of lightning streaked across the sky, followed by a crack of thunder. Bob shuddered and looked up to see clouds covering the sun. The clouds were moving fast, taking on an unusual shape: they formed an image of what looked like an enormous sail boat, skimming across waves upon waves of water. At first, Bob sat there wide-eyed and stunned. "That's it!" he clapped his hands together. "I know what I want. I'm going to buy a boat and sail around the world. That's exactly the change I need!"

Bob decided to stay a little longer on the park bench. He lay down, covered his face with the linen jacket. People chatted and walked by, horns honked, taxi's whizzed, busses rumbled, and Bob fell asleep amidst the cacophony. The big city groaned in the evening sun.

YELLOW BALLOON

Outside today the sky was blue, the leaves were red, and a yellow smily face balloon hung in a tree outside my bedroom window, it's string caught amongst the branches. The smily balloon intrigued me as I arose from a troubled and restless sleep, so I went outside to untangle the string and bring it inside with me.

Where this balloon came from, and how it got there I don't know, but it was just the message I needed to "keep on keeping on," as the saying goes. I won't bore you with the details, but let's just say that lately I'd been feeling a bit "lost in space." And don't get me started on the Netflix *Lost In Space* series. It's a nail-bitter, mind-grabber, sit-on-the-edge-of-your-seat, action-packed thriller! And Dr. Smith is so evil….

Anyway, I tied the yellow balloon to the spare coffee cup on the kitchen table and made myself a cup of the hot brew. I sat at the table and turned the balloon around, looking for any signs from whence it came. I could see nothing, just the two black-inked oval eyes and that huge uplifting smile. I stared at it, and stared some more. It almost seemed like another person, and it made me think of fun times, times filled with laughter and smiles, times I shared with my sweetheart. Of course I knew there would be more to come, but right now he was living halfway across the country helping to take care of his ailing mother. Two months had already passed since he left, and I sorely missed him…. And now I was also on my own dealing with some substantial car and house problems. Sometimes when it rains it pours, I mused, starting to feel sorry for myself again.

I got up to fix another cup of coffee and glanced back at the balloon. Yes, the good times. Remember the good times. I smiled … and the balloon was smiling back at me. I walked over and spun it around. I laughed, a good hearty laugh … and then it popped!

ESCAPE

He sat down, got up, then paced around on the front porch, thinking he had a little bit of time, but not knowing which way to go. Only he, Ralph, didn't have much time at all.

It had snowed the night before, and although the ground was covered in a fresh blanket of white, deep indents of tire tracks that led up to Ralph's cabin in the woods unnerved him. Tire tracks, but no vehicle to be seen; Ralph knew what that meant. They were on to him, but how they had found him, Ralph couldn't fathom. He was so careful, hatching the perfect getaway, going over every detail, plotting his escape for months. And yesterday, after collecting his money hidden in an old peanut can, Ralph packed a small suitcase with everything he would need, including his old red-and-black-checked hunting jacket, a couple pairs of overalls and three flannel shirts, pajama's, a flashlight, various toiletries: toothbrush, toothpaste, a comb, tissues.

He didn't forget food either: packaged cookies, small tubs of applesauce, mini bags of potato chips and cheese curls, juice boxes to wash it all down.

In the middle of the night, he made his escape. Ralph crawled out the window, hot-wired a car in the parking lot, and headed five miles down the road to his beloved haven in the woods. Only it had started to snow, and the car stalled four miles into his journey. Ralph got out and trudged the last mile through blinding snow, suitcase in hand, fingers frozen, slipping and almost falling several times. Finally, he grasped the spare key on the ledge above the door and made it safely inside. Ralph got out of his wet clothes, wrapped himself in blankets and collapsed, exhausted, on the little rickety couch.

The next morning the sun shone lemon yellow, the snow glistened with rainbow flecks, fluffy clouds followed an airplane trail in the sky, crows cawed from the cabin's roof, and Ralph rose refreshed, ready to enjoy the day. He changed into a clean pair of pants and shirt, gobbled down a couple of cookies, walked outside carrying his mini juice carton. That's when he saw the tire tracks.

The old man sputtered, distressed and anxious, choking on his apple juice. Oh, no! They found him.... But where were they? Ralph knew they would arrive any minute to take him back. He sat down, then stood abruptly and began to tread heavily across the front porch. But before he could devise a new strategy, THEY appeared from behind the cabin - his nurse, the security guard, and the managing director of Crest Ridge Nursing Home.

There was nothing else he could do but allow them to accompany him back. A lucid thought flickered through Ralph's mind as the nurse took him by the hand, gently leading him to the van parked behind the tall wall of spruce trees: he wondered if they were finally getting tired of coming to get him. This was his fifth escape.

PRISCILLA

Priscilla Putam graduated Magna Cum Laude from Cambridge University in the U.K. And although she was of both British and Native American descent, she related more to her English heritage than to her ancestry of the Pequot, the Connecticut tribal Indians from the United States. After all, the Pequot had lost a brutal, devastating war against the English back in 1637, with many of them becoming slaves to their captors. Priscilla didn't want to acknowledge this part of her history, or any part of losing for that matter.

With influence due in some part from her mother's parents, who were alumni of this great, historic university, Priscilla received a scholarship to go to Cambridge. Her grades also contributed to her acceptance; she was listed in the top-five of her high school graduating class.

Even before Priscilla entered the institution, she had it all planned out; she knew exactly what she wanted to do: become an architect. As a very young girl, she was fascinated with buildings and houses, and would spend countless hours playing with her Lego set, coming up with new structures that would amaze her parents.

Now, two days after graduating, Priscilla was "off and running," anxious to get her career started on the "fast-track" to success. She had already arranged for several interviews with some of the most prestigious architectural firms in Britain.

As she sat in the corner restaurant, an hour before her first job interview, lost in daydreams of her exciting future, she couldn't know what lay up ahead for her. If she had known, would Priscilla have walked across the street at that precise time? Would she, in fact, have made a different choice. Perhaps, if she had a crystal ball placed in front of her, she would have seen the road her life was going to take.

In the next few minutes, a car accident would leave her bedridden and crippled for the rest of her life. Depression and despair would bring her down; she would feel like a loser, crushed, destroyed, just like her Native American ancestors. It would take three years before a man would come into her life, inspiring her with the words that would change her life: *With courage, anything is possible.* Adopting a different outlook and fresh perspective, Priscilla would then enroll in online writing courses and go on to author many books - fantasy fiction novels - with all of them reaching the Best Seller list.

Yes, it's true that in a quick moment, Priscilla never would become the architect she wanted to be. She lost her physical freedom, became emotionally disheartened; however, she was able to rise above it, find another path, master a different kind of creative outlet and garner a new talent she never knew of or even dreamed she would possess.

PUMPKIN PIE

A generous sized slice of pumpkin pie rests on the paper plate. It's topped off with a big dollop of freshly made whipped cream. Looking really delicious, it's just sitting there on the tall, oak table in front of the old man's house. No one is around when the neighborhood boy walks by with his new puppy and spots the pie only several yards away.

Whoo, that looks good, the young boy thinks. Old man Clark doesn't like anyone very much, and he won't know it's me who took the pie. Without another moments hesitation, he darts onto the man's property, snatches the pie, and runs down the street, while his dog trails behind on a jingling leash. "Oh no!" the boy puffs, "I forgot about all those jingle bells!"

Of course the old man hears the ruckus and bounds out of his house, chasing the little boy down the street, his rubber shoes smacking at the pavement. "Give that back!" he yells. "I'm gonna get you!"

Just as the man seems to be gaining on him, the boy jumps the low white picket fence into another neighbor's yard. The pie falls to the ground and rolls into the flower garden. Quickly, the puppy nabs it and runs to a hole under the front porch, where the boy and the old man now stand together, silently calling it a truce, listening to the *chomp, chomp, chomp* of the pie being devoured by the happy pooch.

GHOSTS

Joe, wearing his traditional *Ghostbusters* tee-shirt, hobbled into the dusty, desert general store gripping a cane. The small grocery and gas station was the place where he and his pals would still hang out on hot summer days. That day they were all surprised to see him arrive limping, supporting himself with a spiral-carved, natural wood walking stick.

"What happened to you?" Bob cautiously inquired, taking note of Joe's deep scowl. "I don't want to talk about it."

"Well, at least give us a hint," Steve said.

"Alright. I was up on the ladder cleaning out the gutters. Let's leave it at that." "Sorry buddy, but at least you're all right," voiced a sympathetic Robert.

"I'm great," grumbled Joe. He shuffled over to the counter and tossed down a couple of bills. "I'll have a bottle of Stewarts Root Beer, Jerry."

"You got it," responded the longtime store owner, who had seen the boys grow up together in the blazing hot, dry town where few people lived and work was scarce.

The friends, now in their late teens, collected their sodas, made their way to the front porch and collapsed onto the four, rusty metal chairs lined up against the storefront. The boys covered their faces as a wind kicked up and blew a whirlwind of desert sand and dried-up cactus blossoms their way. A few customers entered the store; most people the boys knew, along with some passing motorists, traveling down the only road through town, on their way to somewhere else. Everyone was friendly, and more than one person commented on Joe's tee-shirt, saying, "Great movie....Who ya gonna call? Ghostbusters!" Everyone laughed.

However, there were many times in private when Joe's friends made fun of him over his love and obsession with the film. They'd shake their heads, roll their eyes, sarcastically say things like, " You really believe in ghosts?" And, "I hope you didn't find a ghost in your bedroom last night." Or, "*Whoooo*, I'm scared." In fact, Bob had already considered making another joke today, since Joe had on the shirt again, but he decided against it. No point in talking more about sore subject.

The day started to wind down, and Joe, Bob, Steve and Robert continued with conversation about old movies, recent and past sports scores, their favorite team players, plus some of the other little happenings going on around town.

They were interrupted, startled actually, by the sound of a loud, rumbling engine. A bright red sedan, with a misty face of a woman and an eagle painted on it's side, roared into view. As it passed by the store, the car suddenly jolted up, high into the air about fifty feet. No one could see anything in the road to cause it to rise up like that. It just shot up in a flash, like a launched rocket, and just as quickly dropped to the ground, landing on it's wheels and racing off.

For a moment no one said anything. Then everyone yelled at once, "Did you see that!" They looked at each other in disbelief, as the car disappeared over the hill in the distance.

Joe pointed to his shirt, and nodded his head as if to say *Now do you believe?*

THE PARK

Roger snapped his fingers, while Joan swayed in time, singing along with the bluegrass band. It was a hot summer's day and the small town community was invited to a musical benefit in the park to support *Toys For Tots*. Joan, a retired kindergarten teacher, persuaded her busy accountant husband, Roger, to join in the festivities and help raise money for a good cause.

It wasn't long before Roger was enjoying himself too - thus the snapping of fingers. However, after a little while he began to tire in the heat and suggested they go over to the hot dog stand, where they bought two big chili dogs with all the works: extra cheese, onions, topped with a hefty portion of piping hot, three bean chili. They sat at a red painted picnic table, in the shade of two tall oaks, enjoying their lunch, sipping from frosty cold cans of ginger ale and coke.

After swallowing their last delicious bite, Joan asked Roger if he wanted to see one last band before they went home. Roger agreed, and they leisurely strolled back toward the bandstand.

Standing amidst the audience, Roger and Joan began to snap and sway to the beat again.

Someone off to the right called out, "Joan? Joan Oatley, is that you?" Joan turned and there, not far away, was her old college roommate, Alice. They hadn't seen each other in years, and although they had been bridesmaids in each other's weddings, time and distance had pushed them apart. Alice didn't look the same, but Joan was clearly able to recognize her distinctive low toned voice.

"What? Oh my God, Alice! What are you doing here!" Joan shouted above the band. Alice skirted the crowd, moving in close to give Joan a big hug.

"Larry and I moved to this cute little town two months ago. We absolutely love this place." "I had no idea; it's been so long. How many years now?"

"It must be at least forty." Alice shook her head in disbelief.

"Alice, you remember Roger." Joan stepped back to allow Roger to come through. He shook Alice's hand and they all decided to walk out of the park together, talking about some good times they had back in the day. Joan was more than pleased because except for having Roger in her life, since retirement she'd been feeling lonely and now had a new-old friend to talk to and get together with.

OUT FROM THE COLD

Coreen came from Minnesota to New Mexico to stay at the RV park for the winter - her prized, Revelle violin lay in its case on the front seat beside her. She didn't carry much more in the back seat of her old, midnight-blue Toyota: a suitcase full of clothes, a bag of groceries, dog food, and a case of water. Her beloved cocker spaniel, Rooster, lay on his favorite green plaid wool blanket on the floor. Coreen didn't have much of a plan for herself; all she knew was that she wanted to escape the fiercely cold, brutal winters of the Midwest. Not to mention the long brutal hours she spent slaving away at her hometown supermarket deli. So she took her savings and decided to try something new.

After arriving at her rented trailer, Coreen fed Rooster, unpacked her luggage, then decided to change into her new, beige, green and pink floral dress and brown leather cowboy boots stitched with a pink and red rose. She'd start off with a night on the town and take the fiddle with her, maybe see if she could find someone to play with, or even play alone if she was allowed to.

Down the street was Adelaide's, it's multi-colored neon sign blinking in the large, wood- framed window. A country restaurant. Perfect! A couple walked by and entered the restaurant; Coreen followed them in and found a table in the corner facing the large room. She ordered a glass of Pomegranate Iced Tea.

Slowly sipping on her drink, Coreen glanced about, taking in her new surroundings. She noticed several attractive, young women, sitting not far away, chatting amongst themselves. There were a few other couples, and some men wearing cowboy hats, sitting around a large table, laughing and telling jokes. A guitar player, tall and muscular with thick wavy blond hair happened to be setting up his sound system on a small, carpeted stage. There was a relatively large dance floor in front of him.

21

Seeing a possible opportunity right there in front of her, Coreen got up from her chair and eagerly approached the musician, asking if she could play along with him.

"Well, I don't know." He sounded reluctant. He bit down on his bottom lip, shifted his weight from side to side, and then after pausing a few seconds, said "On second thought, let's see what you can do. You can open with a few songs and if I like it, I just might have you join me for all the bookings I have lined up."

"Really! That would be great!" Coreen could hardly believe this was happening.

"Yea, I had been thinking before about hiring another musician. A fiddle player might be what I need."

To say that Coreen was thrilled was putting it mildly. Ten minutes later she was up on stage, smiling, introducing herself, adjusting the fiddle under her chin, picking up her bow. She played several well known songs with impeccable precision and bubbling exuberance including "Take Me Home, Country Roads" and "Ring Of Fire," and "Born To Run." People got up and danced, and after a big round of applause from an appreciative audience, the guitarist walked over and gave her a welcoming hug.

"You're in," he said. "Rehearsals start Monday. That is, if you want the job?"

"I'd love to have this job! Thank you! Wow, this is great!" "I'm Cory." The musician shook her hand.

"And I'm Coreen. Hey, that's funny."

"Yes, it is." He blushed, gave her a big smile. "Okay, well I have to go up now. Stay if you can and watch the rest of the show."

"Be glad to." Coreen settled into her chair, her mind a flurry of warm, fuzzy sunny sparks.

And in that evening, on her very first day in the western town, Coreen had turned the page to an amazingly exciting, brand new chapter in her life. Who knows where it would take her. The adventure had just begun.

WHITE MOON

The white moon sat high in the blue sky. Wind chimes from the house next door tinkled in the gentle breeze. Spring had arrived, the daffodils and tulips were blooming, and the sun's warmth all but chased away the morning chill: it was the perfect day. Sitting in the breezeway of our brand new home, I watched as a family of three rode up the street on their bikes. When they had peddled up to the front of our house, the little girl in the pink bike helmet whistled for her parents to stop. She needed a rest. They all looked tired, so I hollered out, "Hello!" and invited them over for some lemonade.

"Sure, that sound's great," the Mom said as they walked their bikes into the driveway.

While I went inside to make more lemonade and fill three extra glasses, Jack pulled up the extra pink cushioned wicker chairs and kept them entertained around the patio table. Then, I passed around the refreshing drink, topped with lemon slices, along with some of my homemade blueberry bread, as we chatted and learned some interesting things about each other. They were from back East, also recent arrivals to the wide open spaces of the West. Andrew was in Engineering, but had given it up to come here for a dream - to open a bakery. Nina was glad for the change of pace, happy to start a new business with her husband. Kelly, the little girl, wanted to be a bike racer. We shared more stories and everyone agreed that our intentions and goals were to keep moving forward, take time to explore and enjoy life, stay away from the ordinary. It was a new day and exciting experiences lay ahead for all of us.

Suddenly, the little girl choked out, "Mommy!" She tottered, muscles jerking, then collapsed, falling off her chair and down onto the hard cobblestone pavement.

"What's wrong!" I jumped up.

"Call 911!" Nina yelled, bending over the convulsing little girl, cradling her head from further bruising. I raced to my phone and made the call, while her mother struggled to remain calm. "We hoped this wasn't going to keep happening. She's been having seizures lately and they've been getting worse. The doctor couldn't find anything. He doesn't know what's causing them!"

The shrill sound of a siren rose and fell in the distance. It wouldn't be long before the EMS truck would pull up: help would arrive. I rushed back into the house to get a cold compress.

From the bathroom, I heard Nina shriek, "Kelly stopped breathing!"

I ran out to see Andrew getting down on his knees, giving mouth-to-mouth. He kept trying and trying ... and trying. He couldn't resuscitate her. Lights flashed, the ambulance arrived and the paramedics took over. They worked hard, but were unable to revive her either. Kelly, the little girl with the pink bicycle helmet, who rode into our lives not one hour ago, was gone.

Jack and I hugged each other, shocked and horrified, as Kelly's parents, heartbroken and inconsolable, knelt beside their daughter and wept.

The white moon, still high in the sky, watched over all of us.

CEMENT TRUCK

The cement truck rolled around the round-about, it's barrel was painted red, white and blue, and like the flag, there were stars upon it. One can only wonder where the driver was headed, as he traveled down Route 160 in the desert. Perhaps there was a delivery to be made in Gold City for a new foundation on a luxurious home, contracted out by a recently retired couple.... And then who was this driver? Had he been driving this rig for years, carving out a decent wage to bring home to his wife and kids?

Yes, that's it! The cement truck driver has a beautiful wife and four adorable children, ranging in age from three to eleven. The oldest boy is on the little league baseball team, and the whole family goes to watch him play. The youngest daughter takes ballet lessons, and his wife loves to sew. They live in a two-story white-painted house with turquoise trim several miles out from the center of town, and except for the scattered saguaro cactus and mesquite, the land is bare. On some of the neighboring ranches, cattle roam free, and when the wind is just right, you can't mistake that distinct and overpowering odor. It was fifteen years ago when the driver decided not to become a rancher like his father, and he took up truck driving instead. The cement company pays him well, so he takes his wife into town every weekend for dinner and a movie....

Well anyway, as I was saying, the cement truck headed down Route 160; it was at the end of the day. So either the driver was making a late delivery to this soon-to-be new home in Gold City, or he was headed back to his family, where he would sit down to a nice supper of rib-eye steak, roasted red potatoes, and buttered green beans which his wife prepared especially for him - all his favorite of course. And then, to top it off, chocolate cake and vanilla ice cream with sprinkles for desert ... because ... Surprise! Today is his forty-eighth birthday!

OSCARS

Ann Marie's parents let her stay up late one night. That night, many years ago, the Oscars were on television and from that moment on, Ann Marie's life changed forever. The image of a stunningly gorgeous Hollywood actress striding across stage to receive her sparkling gold Oscar amid monstrous applause, burned like fire into her brain. One day *she* would be the one on that stage, thanking everyone for their support and appreciation of her work.

The years steadily passed, and finally the time came when Ann Marie was indeed about to see her dream come true. Seven and a half years after moving to California, Ann Marie was nominated for best actress in *Survival Hearts,* one of the year's most popular, highest-grossing films. For as long as she had wanted this, it still seemed unbelievable, almost too good to be true. Yet, tonight really was that special, wonderful, long-awaited night when - if chosen - fate would see her standing up in the shining lights, all eyes focused solely on her.

Ann Marie took her time getting ready that day, as waves of excitement and trepidation rose within her. She had to win! She just had to! After treating herself to a candlelit bubble bath, Ann Marie carefully dressed in her new, red-sequined gown. It was low-cut, off-the-shoulders, with a tapered waist. Very appealing, she thought, as she stepped into her red satin shoes and eyed herself in the full-length mirror. Just as she swept up the last of her blond curls, in a style reminiscent of the nineteen-forty screen goddesses, she heard the *toot, toot* of the limousine driver pulling up to the front of her new condo. Max, her long-time boyfriend, already seated in the car, greeted her with a kiss. While the limo twisted and turned through lines of traffic on the freeway, Ann Marie sipped champagne and read over her prepared acceptance speech.

Finally they reached their destination, and after stepping out of the black limo, Ann Marie waved, smiled and blew kisses at the cheering crowds. Then she and Max sauntered up the red carpet, posing for pictures and answering interviewers' questions along the way.

Once inside, Ann Marie started to feel lightheaded; the heat of the day and the build-up of anxiety was at last getting to her. She excused herself and carefully made her way to the ladies room. After dabbing the perspiration from her face and drinking a small cup of cool water, she looked wistfully into the large art-deco mirror, the words pounding inside her head: Please! Let me win, I have to win! *Please*! Then, taking a deep breath and gathering her composure, the young actress left the washroom, proceeded to find Max and take her seat.

The show began with television cameras whirling above the audience, thousands of smiles and thousands of hands clapping, followed by an opening number filled with upbeat music and dance. Ann Marie was sitting in an aisle seat six rows back, clasping Max's hand, watching the spectacle unfold before her eyes. It was a while before the announcer approached the microphone with the words Ann Marie was waiting for: "The nominees for best actress in a motion picture are Ann Marie Aimes in *Survival Hearts*, Sandy Wolf in *Readers Game,* Collette Stevenson in ..."

Ann Marie tuned out the rest of the words and waited to hear if her childhood dream would come true. This was it! Would her name be the one called? Would she be the one glamorously

gliding across the stage to receive the highest honors? She held her breath and forced a tense smile.

"And the Oscar goes to ... Ann Marie Aimes in *Survival Hearts*!" Ann Marie let out a shrill squeal as the audience erupted in applause. She kissed the beaming Max, jumped up and hastily ran down the aisle, impatient to hold that beautiful, glorious statue in her hands.

At the edge of the stage, the staircase extended outward to meet her, and without pausing, Ann Marie lifted her leg to the first step. The light shone brightly in her eyes, and as she went for the second step, her shoe caught in the hem of her gown. For a moment she swayed, trying to regain her balance, then down she went, cracking her head against the edge of the hard, wooden stage. She lay there stunned, the audience hushed in shock.

Before anyone could reach her, Ann Marie rose and stumbled up the last few steps, somehow making it across the stage to the podium, a small stream of blood dripping from a gash on the left side of her forehead. The announcer approached her, wanting to accompany her offstage, but she would have none of it. This was the moment she had waited for, for most of her life.

Standing center stage and clutching the Oscar under the harsh, glaring lights, the audience unusually quiet, almost somber, Ann Marie managed to unfold her acceptance speech and began to read. About three lines into it her vision blurred, and overcome by dizziness, she collapsed to the floor, unconscious. Several people, including security and medical staff, rushed the stage; Ann Marie Aimes was picked up, carried off and immediately sent to the hospital, where she was diagnosed with a concussion and ordered to stay overnight for more tests in the morning.

Max came in later, carrying the Oscar and a bouquet of red roses. Ann Marie, looking forlorn and miserable, now wrapped in an drab, grey, unshapely hospital gown, reached a weak hand out to him. In the cold, dreary hospital room, Max walked over to hug her. Ann Marie uttered a heavy sigh, and no longer able to hold back the tears, broke down, her sobs echoing down the halls of the hospital.

MAN ON THE MOTORCYCLE

"This motorcycle could use a soft seat," the man said as he rolled up and parked his black- and-tan Yamaha in front of us. "Can't go fifty miles before my butt aches!" He stretched his legs, preparing to enter the coffee shop for his usual toasted bagel with butter and black coffee. My husband and I had seen him before, though this was the first time he spoke to us.

The day was warm, even in late Fall, so we had chosen a table outdoors where we could enjoy our cappuccinos and frosted cinnamon rolls in the fresh air and sunlight, while admiring the colorful potted flowers on the patio - lantana and lavender, daisies, mums and geranium - and the beautiful golden yellow leaves that floated and spun in the breeze from the Modesto Ash Tree nearby. Well, my husband invited the man to come back out and sit with us. He nodded and five minutes later we three were deep in interesting conversation. He told us he had moved to this desert town six months ago, after his wife died. They were inseparable, and he could no longer bear to be in the house they shared together. So he sold everything, moved west, and took up cycling as his new hobby. He had ridden out to the Grand Canyon, the Painted Desert, Zion National Park and Monument Valley, taking lots of pictures and filling up scrapbooks with his travels. He had more plans coming up too. Next, he would be exploring the Pacific Coast Highway, then on to Oregon and Seattle. We appreciated his stories and told him about some of the places we had been to also, our latest trip being Memphis and Washington D.C. And we didn't forget to mention the huge, and I mean absolutely *huge* pastrami sandwich we got at an amazing deli in D.C.

The afternoon seemed to pass quickly; clouds filled the sky and the sun began to sink behind the hills. I looked at my watch; it was four forty-five, almost closing time. The man got back on his motorcycle, securing the black helmet on his head. "Have a great evening folks" he said as he revved his engine, then took off waving to us before turning out of the dusty parking lot.

We looked for the man on the motorcycle the next time we were in the coffee shop. We never did see him again.

ANTIQUES

Susan loved to shop for antiques; when she wasn't shopping she would think about them all the time. An avid collector, she was able to seek out and purchase many rare finds: a finely carved wooden roll-top desk from the seventeen hundreds, intricate shaped cast-iron coffee grinders and skillets, colorful abstract lithographs from several long gone semi-famous artists, uniquely designed porcelain dolls and figurines from Europe, and various types of vintage glassware, vases, lamps and dishes from places like Tiffany and Carnival.

Without enough room to store everything at home, Susan decided to rent a storage space across town. She hired a handyman to help transfer the items, some too heavy to carry herself. When everything was finally loaded into the 10 by 15 foot temperature controlled unit, Susan was pleased: the room was filled, and everything was safe under lock and key.

The next day, however, a disturbing thought ricocheted through Susan's nerves: what if the handyman, who at one point had borrowed the repository key, made a copy of it? Could she really trust him not to covet any of those unique and precious pieces for himself? Even if he didn't enjoy them as much as she did, he could still sell them and make a tidy profit. Susan became obsessed, more anxious every day at the notion of losing all that mattered to her. She knew she could not live without her treasured possessions. An idea flashed into her fearful mind. She would rent the storage room right next to the one holding her valuables, stay there, and keep an eye on things.

In the adjoining empty space the next day, Susan set up a small cot, brought in a mini TV, a chair, small table, her computer and a couple of valises filled with clothes; from then on, she slept alongside her antiques, with one ear cracked for the slightest sound. Most of her days were spent on the premises too, except for the brief times when she grabbed a quick shower at her old apartment and when she traveled to her brand new job at the office with the big picture window, located directly across the street from the storage space.

SHERIFF

A fitful rain fell, and the Arizona flag and Old Glory, raised high on the silver poles in front of the police station, wildly flapped in the wind, now that monsoon season had begun. The sheriff had just gotten a call that a tractor-trailer had overturned on the Interstate. As he started his engine and pulled out of the parking lot, he struggled to see outside in front of him; the force of fast and heavy water droplets pounding on his windshield almost completely blocked his vision.

Traffic will be backed up for miles by now, he thought. With the siren clearing the way, the sheriff soon arrived at the scene, well before the firetruck and ambulance. Analyzing the accident, he concluded that the brakes on the big rig had failed, and the two men jumped out of the truck as it began to gather speed down the four mile curved portion of the freeway that led to the valley below.

Another police car arrived and the officers began directing traffic. Meanwhile, the sheriff got out his flashlight and weaved his way down the side of the highway, shining the light through the blinding rain and fog. He found the men about a quarter mile from the eighteen-wheeler, now lying on it's side in the left lane of the road. The men, bruised and bleeding, lay in a rocky a ditch. One of them had no pulse; he hadn't survived. The other man was still breathing, struggling to speak, and the sheriff rushed over and knelt down beside him, the distant, flashing lights of his vehicle reflecting dimly in both their faces. The sheriff took his hand and leaned in closer.

"Please tell my wife that I love her. I never told her enough; I wish I had. Tell my girls I love them too. Tell them to do good and make something of themselves."

"Yes, I'll do that," the sheriff assured him, "but please try to pull through." The man squeezed the officer's hand, gasping for air. Then his eyes closed and his breathing stopped.

The sheriff wiped tears from his eyes, as the fire truck and ambulance arrived. What really made him even more sad, was knowing that five hundred yards ahead of where the truck overturned, there was a sign for a runaway truck ramp, where the rig could have pulled off and come to complete stop.

VIVID SWEETENER

"Knowledge is a vivid sweetener." I sipped my coffee - unsweetened - and stared at the phrase printed in the specialty coffee magazine on the table in front of me. Then I overheard two women sitting a few chairs away: "At the retreat, the featured speaker shared his goals with us. He hopes to get five million people meditating five minutes a day for peace on this planet. He believes that will make a huge change for the better," one woman said to the other.

I sat back in my chair, pondering the words - printed and spoken. Yes, that is sweet; if everyone had access to this knowledge, really believed in and took the time to meditate ... well, wouldn't that be something. The whole world would shift, and perhaps even peace would be possible.

Fifteen minutes later, I stepped out of the coffee shop into the bitter cold, quickly zipped up my coat and started for home. It was a short walk down a tree-lined street filled with city apartments, some five stories high. Lights were coming on as people were arriving home from their nine-to-five jobs in early December. In Washington, D.C., many people in my area had government jobs, and you could often feel the unrest as the stress levels rose, with political parties and partisans constantly taking sides against one another. In fact, my job was just as anxiety ridden, and I had needed to take the day off just to clear my head and try to think rationally. As harried workers rushed past me, I continued to muse over all I witnessed in the coffeehouse.

When I got home, I fixed a big dish of vegetable-laden pasta - comfort food I felt I deserved.

Then I turned on the TV. In just a few minutes, I realized that was a mistake; there was more arguing among the people, a hurricane was about to hit Florida, thousands of jobs were lost at a global marketing company, and an army was in the midst of quelling a riot in Asia.

I shut the television off and just sat in the silence. After a while, an idea popped into my head. Why not start with me? I would do something to make a difference. I got out my colored markers and made a sign. I knew that my friend, who managed the Community Center, would let me have use of the building anytime I asked. And tomorrow I would print hundreds of the posters and hang them up all around the city: "WORLD PEACE MEDITATION - SATURDAY, 3 PM AT THE COMMUNITY CENTER."

I only hoped people would show up.

"THE GREAT SHOE STORE ROBBERY"

The judge may have given up on me, but I didn't.... It was a dark, foggy night when I exited the courtroom, still mulling over the proceedings that had been going on all day. *Day One* and already things didn't look good. I could see it in the judge's eyes as he shifted his gaze back and forth between me and the witness, or so everyone believed.

Unbeknownst to all, of which only I was aware but unable to convince anyone, was that this "witness" was a con artist, there to implicate me for a crime I did not commit. They called it "The Great Shoe Store Robbery." Sometime very late at night, someone had broken the glass of the Nina Ricci showroom and ran off with a full load of the Fall line of woman's footwear. I happened to be in the wrong place at the wrong time, while taking an after-midnight walk in hopes of combating my insomnia. The cops, instead, nabbed me, and a witness came forward to claim I was the one she saw breaking into the shoe store. It was starting to look like I would be behind bars for a long time.

Now, as I trudged home after a long, tiring day, ready to face another sleepless night, my mind spun, trying to come up with the perfect, concrete plan to get the charges dropped. After fixing a cup of spearmint tea, I flopped onto the bed, my thoughts still in a frenzy, refusing to believe it would end this way. I would not give up. There had to be something I could say or do to convince the court that I was not the culprit. Maybe going for another nighttime walk would clear my head, help me see a new angle, assist me in building a stronger case for the following day.

I pocketed my cell phone, locked my apartment door behind me, and soon started a moderate pace down the sidewalk, passing by the quiet buildings and empty stores in my upper east-side neighborhood. I felt safe, after having lived here for over three years in this upscale, well lit area, regularly patrolled by security police.

Just then, I heard a crash. A window shattered at the Louis Vuitton store up ahead, on the other side of the street. In a flash I bolted across the street, just as a shadowy figure ran into the store. I followed the robber, being as quiet as I could, even while stepping over the broken glass. With my cell phone camera poised for the shot, I waited until I was close enough to the criminal

- already stuffing piles of shoes into a huge garbage bag - and then I yelled, "Hey! You!"

The thief turned; it was her! It was the "witness." I snapped several pictures, one after the other. Then I ran out of the store, pointing the way for two police officers who were fast approaching.

Caught in the act! These pictures were just the proof I needed, not to mention the added testimony of the officers. Now I knew I had won. The judge would see clearly and close the case, the con artist crook would go to jail, and I would be released. My worries were over.

"SHIP OF FOOLS"

We were like a "ship of fools" thinking we could travel across the country in just two days. After all, we had just graduated college and "the world was our oyster" - this trip would be "the best thing since sliced bread." Okay, enough of the idioms; but seriously, my three friends and I thought a road trip would be just the thing to celebrate our newfound freedom from the books, the tests, the stress and pressure of four intense years of laboriously hard work. And with all of us taking turns driving, we figured we could make it from Boston to L.A. in no time. What we didn't count on were the several mishaps that occurred along the way.

Two hours into our drive, there was a loud popping sound; it was like a small explosion - the left rear tire blew out. We managed to pull over to the side of the highway and call *Triple A* for a tow. Well, it seemed that before we left, Marsha forgot to check under her trunk for an extra spare tire. I don't know how she could *forget* something like that, but at that point, there was nothing we could do. So we were delayed longer than we hoped, because Marsha had to special order a new tire for her vintage Plymouth Colt. Still, we had a good time staying at a roadside motel. Terry, the ever-kind soul, thought to pack plenty of snacks, snacks from chilled strawberries to cheese-curls, and the four of us watched old movies on the small-screened TV. In fact, one of the movies we watched was *Ship of Fools*, which is how I started this tale … only, in our case, we weren't on a boat heading for Germany back in 1933. Thank God! Okay, I digress….

Back to our college cross-country road trip. The next mishap occurred when we got pulled over by a state trooper in Shamrock, Oklahoma. He said we were speeding, and Sue, who was sitting in the passenger seat, disagreed and starting mouthing off to the cop. He told her to get out of the car, and then she got physical. Sue's been known to have a temper, but this time she went overboard. The policeman slapped on handcuffs, brought her down to the station and threw her in the slammer. We tried to get Sue out, saying we'd watch her, make sure she "behaved," but the cop would have none of it. He was a tough guy; though, eventually he softened and let her out after two days.

Then, in Vegas, we forgot to lock the car doors and came out of the casino only to find that it had been stolen. We sat in that city for almost a week, waiting and hoping the car would be picked up. The deputy found it abandoned out by Hoover Damn.

Well, we were pretty upset by the time we left Vegas. We couldn't believe the kind of luck we were having on this trip, so none of us thought about getting gas until we ran out and got stuck somewhere in the Mohave Desert. A kind stranger came by a few hours later, or maybe it was a few minutes later; I don't know. Anyway, he happened to have a spare can full of gas, which got us over to the next service station.

When we finally got to L.A., it was two weeks later.... And then somehow, all the troubles and setbacks we had along the way just "faded into the woodwork." Yes, more idioms, I just can't help myself. But seriously, our time in California was everything I ever could have dreamt it to be: warm Pacific winds, cool ocean waves to splash in, flaming sunsets, long walks on

sandy beaches, special moments watching sailboats glide over a star sparkling sea, balloons floating up to the sky from laughing children, cookouts at dusk, dancing at midnight, sitting at a seaside restaurant eating lobster, scallops and fried clams. All that, and much more.

I was cleaning out my bedroom yesterday and found that old souvenir postcard in a shoebox in my closet. It reminded me of that trip, all those memories. Such crazy fun times. I think I'll call Marsha tomorrow. I haven't spoken to her in years.

FLAME IN YOUR HEART

"I just want to start a flame in your heart." The words echoed in Sarah's head, as she stood on the curb signaling for a taxi, twirling the sparkling, beaded butterfly bracelet around her wrist.

Traffic raced by, her mind softened, relaxed, while she reviewed the evening's amazing events. As executive secretary to the CEO of an investment firm, her responsibilities were many.

And after a week of successfully setting up numerous client appointments and staff meetings, answering endless phone calls, and productively dispensing with the mounds of paperwork laying on her desk, Sarah decided to celebrate her accomplishments: she would go out for a nice dinner at the new restaurant down the street. What better way to end the day - and the week.

Gathering her belongings, Sarah left the office and dodged her way though crowds of commuters making their way home in the bustling city. Fifteen minutes later, Sarah entered the establishment and was greeted by the maitre d', who escorted her to a small table covered in white linen, topped with black linen napkins, shining silverware, and in the center, a crystal vase holding a single red rose. After comfortably being seated, Sarah took note of the rest of the contemporary, upscale restaurant: it was stylishly decorated in gold, black and silver. On walls hung color-coordinated, abstract oil paintings; off to the side was a water feature - a fountain of trickling water running over a compilation of red rocks. There was a gold granite fireplace, and from the ceiling hung several strategically placed black pendant lamps.

Having scanned the menu, Sarah ordered a bowl of ginger butternut squash soup, along with an entree of baked shrimp with lemon garlic butter sauce, grilled asparagus and rice pilaf. While waiting for the soup to arrive, the young woman snacked on fresh baked bread and butter, and constantly glanced toward the door to see all those entering the elegant restaurant. In the back of her mind, she secretly hoped to meet someone interesting.

A few minutes later, a handsome gentleman with dark hair, medium build, dressed in a dark grey business suit and sitting alone on the other side of the room, walked over and asked Sarah if he could join her. Sarah, noticing his attractive features, said okay, and then, to her amazement, a most delightful and stimulating conversation developed. Over dinner, the two found they had a lot in common - from where and how they grew up, to their wishes and plans for the future. They laughed a lot, and Sarah's hopes began to rise; she thought he could "be the one."

They were still in the middle of desert when the young man stopped speaking. To Sarah, it seemed an uncomfortably long time. But that's when he reached for her hand, and leaning towards her, whispered, "I just want to start a flame in your heart."

Sarah went weak; she felt like she was melting into him. She imagined their lips meeting. Shortly thereafter though, and almost too abruptly, he got up, said he had to leave … but not before placing a sparkling butterfly bracelet on her wrist and making a promise to call her the next day.

Sarah stood on the curb hailing a taxi. Deep in her heart, she desperately hoped to see this man again. Then her mind relaxed; *whatever will be will be*, she sang out loud - words her grandmother once imparted to her - as a taxi slowed and pulled up to the curb beside her.

DAY'S TURN OF EVENTS

Austin scratched his head, puzzled at the day's turn of events. Evening had come and glaring spotlights fastened to tall tree trunks brightly lit the ski slopes. As he rode up the ski lift alone, removing his gloves, Austin couldn't quite fathom the circumstances that led up to this particular point in time - sitting on a chair lift at night with skis dangling from his feet, when he had never even skied before in his life. Austin's mind was dazed, jumbled, frantically trying to put all the pieces together, thinking back moment by moment from when the day began. It made no sense, unless ... unless....

That morning, he had gotten into his car to take a short drive over to the Sunrise Diner for his favorite omelet - bacon, onion and white cheddar. The roads were plowed from last nights snowstorm and the sun shone bright, melting whatever residue was left on the pavement. As he sat in the old, worn-out booth waiting for the waitress to arrive with his breakfast, Austin began pondering the documentary he saw the night before about Hedy Lamarr, and how not only was she a beautiful, famous movie star, but she was also an inventor. The movie stated that this actress was the first one to come up with the idea of "frequency hopping," where radio signals are able to "hop in frequency from one band to another." This became what many of our modern, secure communication systems are now based on. Along with WiFi, Bluetooth and GPS.

So it was this morning when Austin pulled into the diner, at exactly eight-thirty am. He knew because he checked his watch before getting out of the car.... The next time he looked at his watch, which was now, it was seven-thirty pm and here he was sitting on a chairlift at a ski area twenty-five miles away. What in the world had happened? Where did the time go, and how did he get over to this mountain slope, sitting on a cold ski chair high up in the air, scratching his head in a mixture of amazement, puzzlement and fear? Then he remembered the Hedy Lamar movie again, and an idea began to form: if you could change the frequency of a radio signal, which was just like tuning from one radio station to another, maybe *HE* could just as well have "changed frequencies," and thus moved beyond space and time to be where he was right now? The questions kept coming as Austin hopped off the lift and began to side step his way down the freshly-packed, powdered slope. Skiers swerved and turned back and forth right by him, but Austin didn't notice. He was busy making a vow to himself, to take up the study of modern physics and quantum mechanics. Someday he would get to the bottom of this and finally know the truth. Someday.

THE WIND

The wind is like a ghost from the past.... I'm sitting alone in the backyard while heavy gusts whistle through the pine and juniper trees, swaying and rocking them along to a hullabaloo of sounds: spinning metal fans, clanging wind chimes, dangling wooden blocks hitting against each other. I hear the chirping of a dozen sparrows. I close my eyes and memories from the past are triggered by these same sounds, the blowing trees, and the wind.

Back then I was alone too, only heartbroken. My husband had left me; I was mourning the loss, and as the wind blew through me that day, floodgates were opened and tears fell in torrents. It was a cleansing, allowing me to begin again.

That was nearly five years ago, and I can't say that things have been all that easy. It took some time to get back on my feet. I bought a car, trained for a new career in social work, adjusted to living alone in a house filled with memories. Things do have a way of moving forward, and you go on, day-by-day, step-by-step.

I also made new friends, visited some beautiful and interesting places - Amsterdam, Vienna, Quebec and Costa Rica. Satisfying work came with the Red Cross, and I was able to assist many families in need. I read books to children in Haiti orphanages, and it was last year that I adopted a child of my own. Her name is Carolina; she's almost two years old now, inside taking a nap.

She's a precious little thing, with curly black hair and such a sweet smile. I know I can do a lot to help her.

Yes, my life has changed greatly since then - since the heavy gusts of wind, the sadness and heartache, the loss, the blowing trees, the chimes, the sparrows ... the wind.

ARTIST

The retro artist's studio was now in shambles. He had rented the small shack on the outskirts of town a year ago today, and while initially Gerard got off to a good start - producing and even selling a few pieces of artwork - sales had eventually dropped off to zero. Having no other income, or skills to obtain an income, stress had taken it's toll on the fifty-five year old man with thin, greying hair. And today, since his lease was up, Gerard would be unable to continue paying rent, thus being forced to vacate the premises.

As he walked into the space wearing his trademark paint-speckled jeans and navy blue ski cap, the disorder and disarray in front of him was even more apparent. Paint cans everywhere, empty ones too. There were brushes and balled-up papers strewn across work benches, mounds of canvas' and cardboard lying in a jumbled heap near the walls, jars of muddy water, piles of rags, random stacks of old newspapers in the middle of the floor, dirt and paint splotches smattered all over the room.

Gerard stood motionless and numb; his mind returned to a dream he had the night before. In the dream, he was standing in the studio - now neat and clean - painting a huge canvas in a completely new style. The colors were unusually rich and vibrant, and the subject matter, unique. There was a knock on the door, and when the visitor entered and saw his artwork, he loved it, demanding to buy it on the spot….

Gerard let out a deep sigh, thinking he wouldn't ever see *that* dream happening. He grabbed a broom and began the long tiring job of cleanup, but didn't get very far before he heard a loud thumping on the door. This startled him so much that he jumped and nearly fell over the paint cans on the floor behind him. With his heart sinking even lower, Gerard prepared to face the landlord, who would now see what a mess he had made of the studio.

Opening the rusty-hinged, wooden door, he was surprised to see a young man in a brown, double-breasted suit carrying a briefcase. "Are you Gerard McDonald?" he asked politely.

"Yes, can I help you?" Gerard answered despondently.

"I'm Lewis McClinsky, and I represent your aunt's estate in Oregon. May I come in for a moment of your time?"

Gerard let him in, embarrassed that this man would see the untidy room. They zigzagged through the clutter and sat at the makeshift table under the dusty, cobwebbed window.

There was a pause and then the lawyer spoke, "I'm sorry to say that your Aunt Lily passed away last week ... but it seems she left you a great sum of money. You will be receiving a check for seventy-five thousand dollars."

Gerard froze, then shook his head and adjusted his glasses. He wasn't sure he heard this right. "Come again?"

"Your Aunt Lily left you money in her will. I just need you to sign some papers and the money will be yours."

It still took another few moments for the news to sink in; then, in it's place, a growing well of excitement. "You mean seventy-five thousand dollars is mine? That money is mine? You're not kidding?"

"No, absolutely not. Here's a pen. Just sign these papers."

Gerard was so happy he could have hugged the lawyer; in fact, he did hug the man, knowing his troubles had vanished and he could now keep his precious art studio.

TUMBLEWEED

Theresa snatched up the tumbleweed from the middle of the dirt road and hurled it over the barbed wire fence. A dove sat close by in a mesquite tree and watched. It looked like she was angry, but that was not the case.

Theresa had recently arrived home, back from a triathlon where she placed first in the rugged event. And although initially ecstatic beyond words, she soon became annoyed with the press, who constantly spent their time hounding her. Yes, it's true that at first Theresa did enjoy all the attention, especially from the businesses who wanted her to promote their products. They had plans to put her picture on the front of cereal boxes; there was also a make-up and cosmetic deal, and she would be appearing in television commercials to promote the newest athletic shoe. How great was that! Famous and rich!

Today though, finding herself with the rare opportunity to walk down a country road alone, Theresa was beginning to appreciate the true meaning of privacy, of being on her own. It was then she saw the tumbleweed. Without thinking, she reached for it, flinging the tumbleweed far and fast. When Theresa saw it land on the other side of the wired fence, something changed in her ... shifted.

All of this - this life - was not what she wanted after all: people chasing after her, always wanting something from her, waiting outside her house for inappropriate photos, going through her garbage can, even starting to print lies about her in the tabloid newspapers and magazines. They were tying up her time, using her for their own self interests, without even taking the opportunity to know or like her for who she really was. No, this wasn't for her. Theresa wanted freedom. She wanted to be free, unobstructed by shackles, ripped away from the chains, unencumbered, just like the tumbleweed that rose high over the barbed wire fence. Yes, she would be just like that. A tumbleweed, a free agent ... and walk away from it all.

RAIN

"She's wearing a smile turned upside down," he said to me through the speakerphone sitting on the cluttered desk in my bedroom. It was raining where they were, and where I was too, had been for days, and that didn't help matters. And so, in the cold, damp drizzle of an early Monday morning, Dad woke me with this distressing call. "Can you come down to the valley and visit with your mother? She's upset. She won't eat. I think she needs some company while I go away on business."

I agreed, although somewhat slightly reluctantly, as I was dealing with a lot at the moment: work deadlines, a busted radiator pipe, a relationship that was about to end, and even more, which I won't get into right now. But my parents and I were close, very close, like good friends actually. Usually I visited them every other weekend when we'd have lunch at our favorite restaurants, visit the mall, and sometimes go to a matinee. We also liked to take long walks through the neighborhood where I grew up, and enjoy relaxing afternoons sitting in the backyard under the trees reading our books.

Anyway, I fixed a quick breakfast, briefly tried to catch up on some paperwork, and made a futile attempt at straightening up my apartment before driving down, making it to their house just after two pm. It was still raining heavily when I pulled into the driveway, and I knew something wasn't right: all the lights in the house were on - every window lit up in blinding, unsettling light. Unsettling, because I knew my father was such a stickler for cutting costs on electric bills, not to mention that it was still early afternoon.

Taking out my spare key, I grabbed an umbrella from the back seat and headed up the front steps, quietly letting myself in. Everything was still, no sounds … and then, the rustling of a newspaper coming from the living room. Rounding the corner I saw them, sitting in their easy chairs, my mother's arms crossed, her face crinkled up in a frown. There were sections of newspaper spread out all over my father's lap, and practically full cups of tea abandoned on the coffee table.

"Rosemary, come sit down. We have something to tell you," my father spoke seriously, but calmly, not giving away anything. I made my way to the sofa, slowly sinking into the cushions in visible trepidation, having no idea what they were about to say. My throat was tight; I could hardly swallow looking at the concern painted across my mother's face.

"You won't believe this," my mother began. Her lips pursed and her brow furrowed into even deeper lines.

My father continued after clearing his throat, "We're selling the house. My company transferred me to their offices in Wyoming, and we are leaving in a month. I told your mother that it hardly ever rains in Wyoming, not like it does here. But she won't listen; she doesn't want to leave this place, or her friends. Maybe you can talk to her?"

I gulped, the news coming as a shock to my system. I was speechless, trying to take it all in, and the only thought that kept blaring through my head was - What about ME? How do you think this is going to affect ME! I would wait until tomorrow to see if this rain would stop.

ROMANCING UNDER THE STARS

"Are we going to be romancing under the stars this weekend?" the waiter asked the waitress, who was polishing the silverware for the wedding reception that evening.

"Maybe," she replied, knowing full well that her co-worker was only making a joke concerning her new boyfriend. She had recently met this guy online and had gone out on half a dozen dates thus far. All seemed to be going well; so far they both liked each other. But still, deep down, the waitress couldn't get the waiter - this handsome man standing right in front of her - out of her mind. She had actually liked him since they first met two years ago, but he was dating someone else. And the woman never told him of her feelings all the while they were working side-by-side as banquet servers for various parties and celebratory events: weddings, anniversaries, sweet sixteen birthdays, bar and bat mitzvahs, museum board meetings and film festival receptions included.

The waitress had tried to move on from desiring this man; she participated in blind dates set up by friends and even found a few prospects on her own - but nothing had worked. She was still hooked on this waiter: he was the proverbial "tall, dark and handsome" type.

In that huge, almost empty room, with that steward standing nearby, her sister's words began to ring in her head. "Put yourself out there and go for it! Take the risk!" The waitress had heard that advice many times from her already married sibling. Maybe today she would finally be able to take that risk and tell him of her love.

The words kept repeating inside her, getting louder, as she circled the white clothed tables, decorated with deep crimson sashes. She placed the silverware neatly around the gold charger plates, while the young man followed close behind adding wine and champagne glasses to the set-up. The guests would soon be arriving:

everything was almost in place, and time was running out for the waitress to speak privately to the waiter.

Quickly, she turned to face him and blurted out, "You know, I've liked you for a long time, since we began working together. Except, I know you're going out with someone else.... You don't have to say anything. There's nothing to say; I just had to tell you this, once and for all."

The young man was taken aback: he had no idea. And the truth was that although he had been in a relationship for the past year and a half, things had fizzled out and they were no longer together. For whatever reason, he hadn't wanted to talk about it - until now. "Actually, we broke up about six months ago," he replied. "I didn't even know you were interested in me."

"Yes," she stammered, "I've just been afraid to show my feelings … and I thought … you know …" referring to his former affair.

"Well, would you like to go out with me? How about tonight when we get off work?"

The waitress' mouth dropped. She couldn't believe it. "Sure," she whispered. Meanwhile, her heart leapt in elation. She took the risk! She did it! And now, tonight, the two of them could very well be the ones … *romancing under the stars*.

PATIO LIGHTS

The patio lights burned bright, even in daylight. At the Mercury Island Resort, it was all part of the tropical scene, with bathers doing laps or floating in the giant, freeform pool, and young couples resting on teal, tangerine and yellow, cushioned chaise lounges, or relaxing in the steaming jacuzzi. Several small groups of older people sat chatting; some were playing cards and scrabble under striped umbrellas at round, white tables - all this, within patio lights hung high on a colorful wire.

A girl with purple hair wearing short shorts and a tank top, with a large yin-yang tattoo on her upper back walked out from the hotel carrying a book, pausing briefly to adjust her sunglasses. She sat down at an empty table and watched the young married couple next to her playing scrabble. The woman, noticing her vibrant purple hair, asked the girl if she would like to join them; she thought for a moment, then said yes. The couple informed her that a friend would be coming down from his room soon to play too.

The young man arrived, greeted the couple and was introduced to the girl with the tattoo. The game began and pretty soon the foursome became involved in an intense game of words. Wooden squares were placed on the board in rapid pace, a reference book was hastily passed around, and the competition rose to an elevated state. Voices became louder, vehemently defending their positions. An argument broke out; it was hard to say who started it. All of a sudden, the single man took a swing at his married friend, who then responded by pushing the young man's chair over with him in it. Ladies screamed, people rushed over, and the resident doctor was immediately called when the couple's friend passed out after hitting his head on the cement. The doctor recommended he go the island hospital for tests.... The girl with the

purple hair had had enough. This kind of fighting over a stupid game wasn't worth it. She picked up her book and left the patio. And as soon as she was gone, to everyone's surprise, all of the patio lights went out.

GIRL WITH THE BRIGHT BLUE EYES

The girl with the bright blue eyes and pale red beret … Cheryl punched the words into her keyboard, the first half of the opening line to her first novel. Sitting in front of the computer, staring at the almost blank white screen, well it was a good start she thought, but where would she go from here. "Come on, come on," she muttered under her breath. The day was getting late, the minutes sped by, and she had to get something down to bring into her writing class the next morning. Another half hour slipped by … still nothing: writer's block had hit her, big time.

Deciding to get up and stretch her legs, Cheryl wandered to the kitchen of her big, rambling country house and fixed herself a cup of raspberry green tea. Outside the white-framed window, the sun was setting in shades of peach, pink and gold. Talking to no one but the air, she kept repeating, "The girl with the bright blue eyes and pale red beret, the girl with the bright blue eyes and pale red beret …" A light breeze blew through the curtains into the living room as she sat down on her cotton, floral print couch.

After a few sips of tea, Cheryl felt her eyelids getting heavy and placed the cup down on the end table, and as she started to drift off, an intensely cold chill ran up her spine. Startled, she sat up, and there in the dusk of early evening, a misty image of a young girl with blonde hair appeared, not five yards away. She looked to be about six years old and was wearing a pale red beret and had bright blue eyes. The little girl started to play in a sandbox, building a beautiful, elaborate sand castle; she didn't make a sound.

Cheryl sat there stunned, unable to move. Finally, mustering up the courage, Cheryl whispered, "Who are you?" The girl continued to play in the sand. Again, Cheryl said, this time more forcefully, "Who are you!"

The image of the girl dimmed for a second, then appeared brighter, lighting up the room. "I am your alter ego, the one who loves to play and have fun. Write what you know in your heart to be true. Let go, find your joy, experiment, create! I am the girl you used to be. I am the girl with the bright blue eyes and pale red beret."

Suddenly, she evaporated and Cheryl was alone, a slow wave of peace and tranquility washing over her. For a moment Cheryl wondered if she had been dreaming, but as she replayed the child's words the realization was clear: she had been taking her writing much too seriously. All the fun had gone out of it. She exhaled a deep breath as tingles of excitement filled her body. Feeling refreshed, new ideas and interesting possibilities for a detailed story line now began to flow through her.

Cheryl got up from the couch and quickly made her way back to the computer. Tapping away at the keys, she wrote, "The girl with the bright blue eyes and pale red beret sat waiting for me in the schoolyard on that fateful day last summer. She had long blonde hair, wore a red-and-blue plaid, pleated skirt, and after glancing around nervously, quickly waved me over." ... Cheryl's long-awaited first novel was finally underway.

BEANS AND FRANKS

"Do you want beans and franks for dinner?" "It's Christmas!"

"I know that. I just thought …" he grinned.

"Well … okay, why not, it might be fun," she reconsidered.

June and Jonathan were living in their RV, having been asked by their landlord to move out of their rented house - the landlord's kids were coming home from Jamaica and their parents wanted them to live in the house. Since then, Jonathan and June had been traveling five months cross country. They had always wanted to see the states and here was their opportunity. They spent their days sightseeing - visiting places like Abraham Lincoln's birthplace, the Oklahoma Route 66 Museum, and Cadillac Ranch - and nights stopping at various RV parks and national park camp sites. One time they even camped in a fast food restaurant lot overnight. Fortunately a cop didn't come by and kick them out.

Today, they had landed in Roswell, New Mexico on Christmas. Since they couldn't very well make their traditional holiday dinner in the RV, June and Jonathan tried to come up with other ideas. For lunch, they stopped at Dairy Queen - the only place open - and got burgers and ice cream sandwiches. But it was suppertime and they were hungry again. June and Jonathan hoped for something special, but when they looked through the rest of their supplies, all they came up with was a can of beans, a package of franks and some cheese and crackers.

"That'll be interesting," June said. So she lit a candle on the little table and the couple sat down on the little couch, and while soft music played in the background, June and Jonathan talked and laughed, and shared a beans and franks, cheese and cracker Christmas dinner.

CLARA AND ED

The old woman crossed the street carrying a brand new trash can. She was wearing dark shades, even though it was cloudy and the skies were threatening to drop a heavy, cold rain. I was sitting in my car reading a book, waiting for Bill to get out of the doctor's office when I first noticed the woman. I went back to reading only to look up a minute later when I heard a loud rapping on my window. It was the old woman.

"Don't worry. I'm not out to hurt you."

"What do you want?" I answered somewhat gruffly; she startled me with that hard knocking. "I have a baby chick and a duck in here," she said, pointing to the trash can. I found them over there, behind the store. I couldn't leave them to die, and I can't take them home. My husband wouldn't let me keep them."

"What do you want me to do?"

"Could you take them to the shelter? I don't have a car."

I sighed, wondering if I should get involved. Already, I was worried about Bill's health, not to mention my everyday concerns and the piling-up stress of world affairs; I didn't need anything more to think about. "Ah, I don't know," I said, shaking my head.

"Here, look." She lifted and tilted the plastic trash basket toward me, and that's when I saw the cutest little balls of fluff with big sad eyes blinking at me, and heard the sweet *cheep, cheep, quack, quack* registering in my ears. How could I refuse.

"Okay, I'll do it." The old woman opened the car door, placing the trash can in the back seat. "Thanks a lot," she said. "I appreciate you." She shut the door and as I looked back, I could see her skip away, or at least it seemed that way.

Five minutes later Bill came out with good news from the doctor. What a relief. We hugged, and then I showed him the chick and the duck; he thought they were as cute as I did. It was now five-fifteen: to late to take them to the shelter. So Bill and I brought the chick and the duck home for the evening. They stayed with us the next evening too, and then the next. And that's how we ended up with Clara and Ed - a chicken and a duck, two new birds of a feather family members.

RISEN FAITH

Heavy mists of rain rose off the roof like smoke on a burning building. Lightning blazed and thunder cracked and rumbled in rising crescendo, and a spider took cover in the rafters at Isabella and Jim's house. Isabella, who was sitting on the covered front porch watching the pelting rain and deluge of water falling from overflowing gutters, turned to look just as the grey coupe turned up the street and into the driveway. Preacher Jim, Isabella's husband, was just getting back from a weekend spiritual retreat, and she was ready to hear what she hoped would be good news.

Jim Greenwood had been preaching the word of the Lord for the past twenty years, and he had always been pretty confident in his faith, in the ways the Lord worked in and through the lives of the people around him. Many had come to hear his sermons and be uplifted from their suffering and worldly troubles. But within the last year, Jim's convictions began to falter. With the discord upon earth increasing, Jim's hopes for peace on earth were dwindling. He had fallen into despair and Isabella hoped that a spiritual retreat might bring back the positive, lighthearted husband she used to know. What she didn't yet realize was that it wasn't the retreat that lifted Jim's spirits. It was something else, something she could never have imagined.

Driving back that afternoon from the mission, Jim was still feeling down. He was heavily disappointed in the weekend's activities; the speeches and seminars were unable to make him feel better. In fact he was feeling worse: he was facing a crippling loss of faith. An unseen weight bearing down on his chest was making it difficult for him to breathe, and the dense rain made his spirits droop even further.

Lost in a cycle of gloomy thought, Preacher Jim's car entered a foggy area on a small stretch of the deserted country road. There would be another hour of driving before he would reach home, and

Jim was getting tired. That's when he saw a person standing off to the right side of the road, trying to flag him down. He almost drove right by, as the haze was making it difficult to see. But thinking someone was in need of help, Preacher Jim pulled over at the last second to give whatever assistance he could. Perhaps there was a flat tire or a stalled engine up ahead. At any rate, there must be something he could do.

As Jim got out of the car and began walking closer, he stopped, shocked to see this wasn't an ordinary person calling him over. This man, or rather, this being, was about fifteen feet tall and he seemed to glow: there was a shimmering light surrounding him. He was wearing a one-piece blue garment, marked with a strange-looking insignia. He had no hair and his eyes were big, bigger than the average human.

Before Preacher Jim could turn and run back to his car, the glimmering being raised his hand and spoke in a powerful, yet calm voice, "Preacher Jim! I've been waiting for you. I am Vicor, from the Star System A200SolX. You and I have a lot of work to do together … if you so choose."

The minister shook his head, not understanding. What kind of work could they possibly do together? He hadn't yet voiced this thought before Vicor continued, "Many people believe in God, but they are not aware of, or don't believe in the existence of life on other planets. I'm here

to tell you there are many worlds and universes out there filled with life. We are your brothers and sisters and we are here to help, if you ask…. You can, Brother Jim, help to spread this knowledge."

The preacher stood there, shocked by all that he was hearing and seeing. This flew in the face of everything he knew and believed in. Weren't we supposed to be the only planet with life? The researchers and scientists hadn't shown any proof of life elsewhere.

And who exactly was this individual? Could he trust him? Was he an illusion, a hallucination? Was he connected to the fallen angel?

Yet, this entity seemed to be emanating an extraordinarily peaceful and loving energy, quite unlike anything he had ever felt before. Jim felt perfectly safe and protected, amidst all the doubts and confusion his mind produced. "I'll think it over," he stammered, to which Vicor replied, "I'll be in touch for your answer."

Preacher Jim got back in his car and took another look out his window to glimpse the light being, but he was gone. He had completely disappeared. The minister drove the rest of the way home in silence, dumbfounded. This was beyond his comprehension … but, since the world as of late was in even more disarray, with political, economic and religious strife widespread, not to mention some of the natural disasters that were happening, perhaps he and this "Vicor" could be of some help. Maybe open people's eyes to a bigger picture, see how much more there was to consider. A new, vibrant sense of enthusiasm rose up in the heart of Preacher Jim. Waves of excitement traveled through his body as he turned his car into the driveway, exhilarated and ready to meet his wife.

POST OFFICE

Grandma worked at the small town post office in Maine when she first met my grandpa. It was fifty years ago on a bright, sunny day when she stood behind the counter, sighing from boredom. Business was slow and she was looking forward to her lunch break; the image of the ham-and-cheese sandwich waiting for her in the little brown paper bag on the backroom shelf flickered invitingly through her mind.

Bells chimed as the front door squeaked and opened. A young man of about twenty walked in wearing a beige, cotton-weave jacket and matching trousers. Grandma told me she couldn't help but whisper out loud, "Wow, he's handsome!" He didn't hear her, though. She proceeded to straighten her hair and press her lips together, hoping her pink lipstick was evenly dispersed.

"Hello," he said, pulling out an envelope from inside his coat, "I'd like to mail this to Buffalo.

How much will it cost?" Grandma weighed the letter and announced the price. "Didn't bring enough," he shrugged. "Well, I'll come back later."

Grandma acted quickly, "I have some extra money I can let you borrow." "No, I couldn't," he responded.

"Of course you can. Please!" She ran to the stockroom to get her purse. And before the whole transaction was complete, Grandma had politely asked the young man if he would like to share her sandwich as she would be taking a break in a couple of minutes.... Of course, my grandpa didn't fail to notice her nice personality and charming looks either; he was smitten.

They are still together today, after having raised four children ... and now they're enjoying good times with ten grandchildren - all thanks to the pluckiness of my grandma that one spring day at the post office.

TORNADO

I was in my barn, barefoot, when the tornado hit. The sky was just starting to lighten, the dawn of another day, and I had gone out to milk the cows. I was surprised to see a gift basket, along with a thermos of coffee, sitting outside the barn door. It was from one of my neighbors; she left a note apologizing for the disagreement we had the other day in the market.

How nice, I thought, walking into the building on my one hundred acre farm. I kicked off my boots - I don't know why but my feet were sore already. I poured a cup of the still warm coffee and took several swigs. Then I opened the plastic-wrapped basket of goodies. Inside were several pleasant-smelling soaps, a small puzzle, a box of chocolate covered toffee, a package of strawberry tea and a tiny succulent plant.... All was forgiven and forgotten.

I took a bite of toffee and another sip of coffee when, in the next moment, everything grew silent, so eerily quiet ... except for the distressed mooing of the cows. Oh no! I knew what that meant, and couldn't believe I hadn't bothered to listen to the radio's weather report. I usually did too, but this morning I woke up late and was in a rush.

Suddenly there was a roar, like a speeding freight train bearing down on me. Before I could do anything, I, along with the barn and everything else in it, was lifted into the air and flung through space; I landed in a tree at my neighbor's farm, a good distance away, totally amazed I was still alive. Luckily the tree broke my fall, thank God, or I wouldn't still be here today.

Anyway, I slowly climbed down the huge red oak, my ribs aching and bruised, and walked barefoot through the debris, back to my central Kansas home. The house and barn were gone, just a pile of rubble in their place; many of my beloved cows lay unmoving. That was the moment so many years ago, and I will always remember it - standing there crying, clutching my ribs, staring at the devastation - when I decided to sell my property and move ... to French Polynesia.

MILE LONG TRAIN

A mile long train passed through the college town four times daily. Traffic was stopped at the crossroads, red lights flashed and the lowered crossbar prevented any further movement. Minutes ticked by - it was a slow train - and the two friends who waited with backpacks, already late for class, were getting impatient. Finally, the boy with the impulsive temper had enough. "I'm going to jump on this train, so I can jump off on the other side. Are you with me?" he asked her.

"Ahh, I don't know," she replied.

He edged her on. "Come on! Do or die!"

Unwilling to appear "chicken" in front of this boy she admired, the girl reluctantly gave in, though cheerfully said, "Okay, why not." So the two of them made a run for it. The boy leapt first and landed on the bottom rung of the black iron step. He turned back, holding out his hand to reach her, and she, running alongside, extended her arm and up she sprang. Both were now safely aboard and standing on the platform between cars. The boy looked at the girl, a strange expression crossing his face. In the next instant, he had made his decision.

"I'm not getting off," he yelled above the engine's roar. She was dumbfounded. "What!"

"I'm taking this train out of town. I want to see what adventures are up ahead for me. Are you with me? Do or die!"

It didn't take long before she shouted, "Do!" Dropping their backpacks, they sprawled out on the open platform, smiling at each other as the mile long train curved it's way out of town.

Part Two

3RD DEGREE

"What are you trying to hide?" The hard-handed cop grilled the witness sitting on the high- backed uncomfortable wrought iron chair. A light bulb dangled menacingly above the man's head, now bowed low to cover his growing anxiety and concern. The door behind him was locked in the room often used for witness protection cases in the 4th district of Chicago's South Side Police Precinct.

"Nothing ... I told you everything I know."

"Tell me again. You know, we can't protect you if we don't get the facts. We need to bust this gang and we have no other credible leads. You help us, we help you. It's that simple."

The potential witness chewed on the end of his toothpick, then asked for a glass of water. He needed time to think. Should he give the cop all the details, name names, come totally clean?

Either way, it didn't look good for him. Finally he made the decision to talk.

"Alright ... It was Crazy Larry Stanwick. He was down by the dry dock talking to his boss, Gozo Bonaris. I was walking, trying to get some air, as I said before. But I ... I didn't just walk by like I said. I ducked behind this cargo container and heard the whole conversation. Crazy Larry said, 'I just got word that Rocko and his posse are on to us. They heard about the drop from some snitch. I don't know who. But he wants a piece of the action. I think they'll be showing up soon. Take us on by force.' Then Gozo said, 'Nah, I don't think they'll show. And if they do, I can take care of them.' Then Crazy Larry said, 'Best we walk away. I don't want to lose my life over this.' He was sounding desperate at this point. 'Forget it,' Gozo said, 'You're not leaving. You signed up for this deal, and if you walk out now, you know what'll happen to you.' I could tell Crazy Larry knew exactly what he was talking about, because he just coughed several times … sounded like he was choking." The witness gulped down some more water.

"Go on," the cop pressed him.

"Well, it was then that I heard the shots. I took a quick peek out from where I was hiding and saw a bunch of guys in black leather jackets with the red armband and I knew it was Rocko's gang. They let 'em have it. Crazy Larry and Gozo were down on the ground in a matter of seconds. I knew they were gone. I backed up quietly, but I tripped and Rocko heard me. I took off; they started chasing me. I'm sure they got a good look at me. But I was a track star in high school and I soon outran them. That's when you guys saw me running on 104th Street and pulled me in … And that's the whole story. Now, I told you all I know. Can I go?"

"Not yet. We appreciate you help," the cop had softened. "Now, I'm advising you to get into the witness protection program. That's the only way you'll be safe."

"Not interested. I have a life here, you know."

"A life somewhere else is better that having no life at all isn't it? Besides we need you to testify in court. And you know, some aren't going to like it."

"Why should I testify?"

"Because people have died, and more will if we don't put a stop to this smuggling now."

The witness sat back in his chair. He didn't want to end up dead either, so in a minute, the answer was easy. And to make the most of it, he said, "Ok, if you send me to the Bora Bora Ruby and Pearl Beach Resort and Spa, then I'll go."

SNOW

The snow stopped almost as suddenly as it began. Good thing too, because we still had a long way to travel across the plains, then on through the deserts of New Mexico and Arizona until we reached our final stop in Malibu, California. We had been riding for days now in early spring, on bicycles with heavy backpacks strapped across our backs, and we were tired, very tired. We thought it would be fun to travel cross country on a bike, exploring the back roads of the U.S. - a new adventure that would take us away from the rat race, noise and chaos of our everyday busy lives. But what we didn't realize was just how taxing it could and would be. We had just crossed into Missouri when a heavy snow started to fall. It was dropping by the bucketful and I couldn't see Mark up in front of me. My bike started to slip on the snowy pavement, and as I skidded into a fall, I screamed. Mark heard me, turned around and helped me up. I was ok, except for a bruised knee, but I was exhausted, and now there was the blinding snow to deal with.

And then it ceased, just like that, and the air cleared. "Wow, that was weird." I shook off my hat. "I'm cold and wet," I grumbled. "I need to stop a while," and Mark agreed. I scanned the area, "There's a coffee shop up ahead. Let's go there." He nodded, and we walked our bikes up to the restaurant. We decided on a couple of burgers and fries to go with our steaming hot mugs.

Afterwards we pressed on to find the nearest motel and crashed for the night. I didn't sleep well, and the next morning I was up early having serious second thoughts about continuing on with bicycles. "This is too strenuous for me. I'm worn out. And then that snowstorm. I think we should turn back and go home."

"No," Mark protested, "I really want to accomplish this goal. It means a lot to me to keep going. Besides, you'll be glad you did it too."

"But it's too hard. It's not fun for me anymore," I countered.

"Please, for me … and I guarantee you will get a big reward for making this trek."

"Well it better be something good," I muttered, as I shoved the rest of my nightclothes and toiletries into in my backpack. I was still upset. This journey was wearing thin, getting on my last nerve, and I wondered why I even said yes to this trip.

We headed out mid-morning and rode the whole day, probably a hundred miles, stopping only for a quick lunch and snack break. We repeated this routine for more days than I care to remember. I tried to appreciate the things I saw along the way: the colorful birds flying by the side of the road, the occasional deer, wild flowers blooming in nearby fields, red rocks and towering mountains in the distance - but my muscles were aching, my back and butt hurt, along with shoulders sore, tense and tight. I was even getting bleary eyed. I didn't think I could make it much further, but finally … finally we rode up to Venice Beach. I dropped my bike and trudged toward the sparkling water, breathing a huge sigh of relief. Mark came up behind me, wrapped his arms around me and said, "And now for your reward. See this paper. Do you know what it is? I shook my head. "It's the title to our new home. I bought us a place high on a cliff overlooking the ocean. It's a few miles up the coast. I know you've been wanting to get out of DC for a long time, and I wanted to make your dream come true."

"Mark! I can't believe it!" I was stunned. "It's more than I thought possible! And just like that song: '… Impossible things are happening every day.' Oh thank you! Thank you!" We hugged and kissed as the sun began to set, and I was more ready than ever to rise to a brand new day.

A QUAIL'S LIFE

All the quail had felt the heat on that sweltering July day in the desert of the Southwest, and dusk, covering the land in checkerboard shadows was a welcome relief. Jerry gathered his young'uns around him for a family meeting before they'd retire for the night amidst the bushy juniper tree's branches.

Jerry singled out Pete, "You mister, I sent you out on a mission today. Now … what was it?" "It was to find the lady I would settle with, Pop."

"Right. And how did you make out?" "Well … I …"

"You've grown to be a strong independent quail, my boy, it's time you start your own family." "Yes, Pop, I got ya. So, I went across the river today; I know you all know I've had no luck with the ladies around here. Anyway, past the river, past some of those rocky hills, past the last thicket of manzanita bushes. And guess what."

"What?" The rest of the family crowded in closer to hear Pete's tale. Susie, the youngest sat in the dirt at Pete's feet, eager to hear more. It was sounding like he'd had a big adventure that day and everyone was hopeful and supportive of Pete finding a future partner.

"After all that walking and a little bit of flying, I got so tired in the blazing heat that my eyes started drooping and I couldn't stay awake. I lay down under a mesquite tree and fell asleep."

A hush fell over his siblings. "Ooh, what happened then?" Sonny, the second youngest son asked, and everyone nodded along, their topknots bobbing up and down.

" I don't know how long I was out, but something woke me."

"Yes, yes …" Jerry was getting impatient and hoped there would be a good ending to this story. He clucked, "Go on …"

"I felt something on my beak and I opened my eyes. And I'll be darned, standing above me was the sweetest, prettiest, most beautiful quail I ever laid eyes upon. She had the brightest rusty-red head feathers I've ever seen, and her body was the silkiest of grey with rich chestnut colored flanks and white stripes in just the right places. Plus creamy gold and black on her belly. She batted her eyes at me and poked me with her gorgeous head plume."

"Wow! Then what happened?" Sonny asked.

"Don't you know she said to me, 'I just kissed you. Like in *Sleeping Beauty,* except this time it was the girl who kissed the boy and not the other way around.'"

"I remember that story. Mom used to tell it to me all the time," Susie said with a tear in her eye. She was remembering their mother who passed away last year when she had a run-in with a neighboring fox. Jerry had never gotten over the pain of loosing her and he was now trying extra hard to watch over his young and to make sure they were well off, with each entering into a happy home.

"Yes … Mom," everyone cooed, remembering her loving ways.

"Anyway, the rest is history! We are getting hitched tomorrow. So it's *adios amigos*!"

Jerry shook Pete's claw and patted him on the back. "Well done my boy, well done." All five brothers and sisters waddled up to congratulate him. They squawked and jumped up and down at Pete's happiness and success at finding the perfect lady.

TREASURE CHEST

Kevin had a dream about a treasure chest: he was sailing along with his crew aboard a small pirate vessel in search of lost treasure. Kevin was the captain, and although they had set sail from the Spanish seaport three months ago and were just now starting to run out of food, he kept pressing the ship onward, against the protests of the twenty men in his charge. In this dream, Kevin, the captain, had a dream that he found a huge treasure chest filled with gold and silver doubloons in a cave on a deserted island. It was worth a fortune and he would be rich. Hence, he would not give up searching for the mysterious island holding his future bountiful prospects.

Finally, the next day at sunrise, the lookout yelled, "Land ho!" To which, Kevin roared, "Full steam ahead." Three hours later the ship pulled as close as they could to the rocky coast and dropped anchor. Three small boats were lowered and the captain and thirteen men rowed to shore. Once on the island they split up into two's and began combing the island for clues to the whereabouts of the prospective treasure chest. Kevin and his first mate entered the forest to the left and chopped their way through the thick brush. The sun beamed bright though the trees, the air was hot, and the men were soon dripping in sweat. Kevin stopped to wipe his brow and thought of the cave. He knew it would be covered over with long green lush vines, and there would be a noticeable crack in the rock, shaped like a crescent moon, on the lower right hand side of the wall. It wasn't long after that when they came upon that exact vision the captain had seen in his dream. They ran to the vines and pulled them aside. And there, indeed, was the cave with the crack in the wall, it's oval opening leading into the darkness beyond. The first mate lit a flame and they entered, their bodies filling with excitement. They wove their way around several twists and bends, dodging hanging spiders and scurrying lizards, until they found a small circular room. In that space sat the old wooden chest, three feet tall and three feet wide. The two rushed forward to ply it open, and lo and behold, it *was* filled to the brim with the valuable coins.

Shouting in joy and laughing at their good fortune, they dug their hands deep into the shiny piles of loot, gathered up the coins and flung them into the air above their heads. The coins crashed landed all around them, with several landing on Kevin's head. *Bang! Bang! Bang!*

Bang! Ring! Ring! Ring! The phone was ringing and Kevin woke up from his dream about the treasure chest. He rolled over and reached for the receiver. "Hello?"

"Hey, Kevin. Did I wake you?" The man went on before Kevin could get a word in. "This is Ray. You know, your brother?" Ray liked to make jokes about the obvious, to which Kevin just shook his head and grumbled.

"What do you want, bro?"

"I just got a call from our cousin, Sue, the one we haven't heard from in a few years. Our Uncle Bill died and it seems he left you a small fortune. We all knew you were his favorite nephew, so it's no surprise to me, though I can't say Sue sounded all that happy about it.

Anyway, she wants to meet with you next week.... And hey, I'm thinking Kev, if you want to throw a few pennies my way, or even some big fat dollars, I'll certainly be glad to take 'em."

Kevin let out a loud laugh. Then he threw the phone high up in the air, shouting *Whoo Hoo*, bowled over at having such a prophetic dream and the sudden riches.

GUMBALL MACHINE

It was after midnight when the movie let out, and as I exited into the lobby, still feeling uplifted and transported to another world - the magical movie world - I noticed a gumball machine in the corner near the door. *Why not have a little more fun?* I thought. I wandered over to the machine and placed fifty cents in the turnstile, which instead of gumballs, held little plastic spheres containing rings and necklaces, stick-on paper tattoos, tiny bouncing balls and little troll dolls. *Click, click, click* and a troll doll rolled down the chute - a little elfin man dressed in a white T-shirt and black pants.

Prying open the sphere I retrieved my prize, but then noticed a tiny folded-up piece of paper at the bottom. I unfolded the thin sheet and read the perplexing message: *Congratulations!*

You're one in a million, the only one to receive this valuable set of instructions. Use it wisely and all the world will see a better place. Hold this troll in your palm and count backward from ten.

Well, first I laughed; it had to be a joke .... On second thought - and perhaps I was still lost in movie magic - maybe there was something to this. Stranger things have happened. As I walked out into the night air, I paused under a streetlight and decided to give it a try. After all I did want to see a better world, a peaceful world. No one was around, so I shut my eyes and counted down from ten. I kept thinking of a peaceful world where everyone was happy. When I reached *One*, there was a peculiar rush of wind that almost knocked me off my feet. It lasted about ten seconds and then stopped. I was overcome by a joyful, yet serene feeling. It was like a silence, a stillness inside, unlike what I'd ever felt before, even when the loud rumbling of the subway train below the grate next to me began to roar. I started to walk and there was a certain lightness in my steps, a sense of weightlessness which also stuck me as highly unusual. Could this wish have worked after all?

After a good night's rest, I was back on the subway ready for another day's work at the law firm. I was anxious to see if the previous night's incident had any effect on the rest of humanity. I was still feeling really good and hoped there might be a change in others too.

And it did seem like people were acting nicer, more congenial and caring. I noticed two strangers sitting side by side in the subway car and one of the girls spilled her coffee on another's pale-yellow spring jacket when the train jerked. "It's fine, no worries," the girl said. And she reused the offer to have it cleaned by the girl who spilled the coffee. Then at work, the manager called one of the secretaries into his office. He had to let her go, and even though she had tears in her eyes, she told me she understood, that it was okay and would soon be looking forward to finding something else. Later on my lunch break, someone cut in line and no one said a word.

After several more interesting and good things happened, I was beginning to believe that things in the world really were changing for the better. The wish with the troll was working.

After work I decided to take the bus home and walked a different route to get to the bus stop. I saw a noisy crowd up ahead and crossed the street to avoid it. People were yelling and carrying signs - picketing their low wages at the fast food restaurant. Just as I passed by violence broke out. Someone threw a brick and smashed a window. Protesters began tussling with police, resulting in the demonstrators being handcuffed and thrown in the back of police cars. I hurried on my way and just before I reached my stop, I glanced in the window of a restaurant to a

television on the wall and saw the latest news. Bombs were being dropped in the Middle East and people were fleeing the area. Chaos and disorder reigned.

Well I didn't need to see any more bad things to know that the world hadn't changed after all. What was I thinking? That troll and it's stupid instructions were some kind of cruel prank. When I got home I headed straight for that troll and flushed him and the instructions down the toilet. I wished I never saw that gumball machine. I must have been crazy thinking things could be different, believing in peace - world peace - believing in the impossible.

Sprawled out on the couch, feeling under the weather and that all hope was lost, I couldn't know, would never know an important detail I completely missed. On the back of the tiny instruction sheet, which I failed to turn over, was printed the following words: *The countdown and visualization must be repeated two times a day for two months. If this is done, your dreams, goals and ideas will take full effect. It will work. It is guaranteed. It is so.*

WISP OF SMOKE

A wisp of smoke rose from over the ridge in the distance, and that was the moment Claire made the snap decision to circle back in the rented two-seater Piper Cub she was piloting alone on the hot mid-August afternoon. This thin string of smoke could potentially turn into a dangerous and fast-growing forest fire. And Claire, the gal who'd always be the one to lend a helping hand, took it upon herself to go down and investigate this likely looming disaster.

Shifting gears and maneuvering an easy turn, the thirty-something woman flew over the mountain peak and saw the point where gathering smoke rose from the valley below. Claire radioed for help, but all she got was static. She tried again, jiggling the wire, but it was no use - the radio had somehow died. Claire was nearing a state of panic but she took the aircraft low and managed a loud bumpy landing in the field not far from the bright orange flames that licked at tall brown grasses and small mesquite bushes. She was jittery from being jostled in the landing, and of course from nerves, but still intact. Claire had no particular plan in mind. There was no water, except for a couple of 32 oz plastic drinking bottles she thought to pack. She looked around the back of the plane and saw five folded blankets, probably left there from the previous pilot. Maybe that would do. She could throw the blankets over the flames, try to snuff it out.

Claire grabbed the pile and headed off to attack the flames. Throwing one blanket over a small patch of flame, she managed to stamp out the threat. But then she looked around and saw several other small fires nearby, and they were getting bigger by the minute. What to do? Claire ran to the next and extinguished it, though it was becoming clear that she would never be able to put out all these fires by herself. Smoke was rising and filling the area. Soon Claire was lost in a swirling grey cloud, unable to see clearly. She began to cough uncontrollably and was forced to back away, unable to handle the thick heavy fumes and heat of the flames. She had gone maybe 30 yards when she collapsed in a heap, passing out on the dry brown grasses in a sea of chaos and imminent peril.

When Claire opened her eyes, everything around her was blurry. She detected a movement off to her right and then somebody was adjusting something on her face. An oxygen mask. "Hey Mike, she's coming to," a voice called out to someone else up front driving a vehicle. An ambulance. "She's going to be alright."

"Where am I? What happened?" Claire barely whispered.

"The ranger found you and radioed for help," the paramedic said. "You were out by the fire and could have died. I'm not sure why you don't know this but we do controlled burns out here on a regular basis. It helps protect against potentially more destructive fires when we keep the vegetation trimmed down and in check. I'm surprised you weren't aware that we were doing a couple of prescribed burns today, seeing as you were piloting a plane."

"I just moved here a few days ago from Delaware. We have burn bans but I thought ..." "What's your name?"

"Claire."

"I'm Bill. Well Claire, your lucky to be alive." The medic took her hand into his. "And if you want to say it's anything like the song *Luck Be A Lady,* then you're one lucky lady today."

Claire gazed up into Bill's deep blue eyes and sweet smile, and a wafting image, a wisp of future couple possibility flickered and danced through her mind.

LATE NIGHT TRAVELS

Gravel crunched under the tires as we pulled out of our driveway at the eleventh hour. I didn't know it at the time, but deep down Ronald was pretty angry. Yes, things hadn't been going so well in his life for quite some time, but somehow he managed to keep it all hidden from me. Out of work for a while, repressed emotions had built up - intense feelings of frustration and anger.

So it was dark and the stars were out when he said, "Let's go for a ride. I need to get out of the house." Of course I wanted to please him, and even though it was late and past my bedtime, I said yes. After all I did want him to be happy, and I thought he was, sort of. Although I must admit he had been acting a bit strangely over the last couple months. Several times I saw him pacing circles around the kitchen island, and when I asked him about it, he said he just wanted to get some exercise. I also noticed him cleaning and throwing out a lot of stuff he had collected over the years - some of his prized possessions too, like his valuable antique camera and rare vintage movies. And he was sleeping extra late in the mornings too. Then last Saturday, he insisted on seeing the *Don Quixote* movie playing at the cinema, knowing full well it was the ballet version, even though in the past he voiced a dislike for ballet. I absolutely enjoyed the ballet though, the dancers were beautiful, their grace and execution of movement perfect.

Ok, so it was at the eleventh hour that we backed out of our driveway, tucked in our warm winter coats and wooly gloves. Speeding down the dark country road under the ebony sky I was a bit nervous, not sure where Ronald was taking us. There were twists and turns in the road and if anyone didn't know the road well, they could easily have made a wrong turn. Luckily Ronald had traveled this road many a time and was an adept driver. He had even driven a bus for tourists back in the day. As a bus driver, he worked for a company that set up trips for people to visit famous local landmarks, attend dinner theatre productions, spend an afternoon at the casino.

Ronald turned on the radio, blasting the song that was playing - *Symphony No. 9 (Ode to Joy)* by Beethoven. I sat back in the seat letting the music wash over me, trying to stay calm with his somewhat erratic driving. For miles and miles we rode in the moonless black night. Eventually the radio was turned off and all was silent except for the steady humming of the engine.

I was getting ready to ask Ronald to turn back when a bright light from a car's high beam shown through the back window. It was unusually luminous and I turned around to get a better look. It was then I realized the light wasn't from a car after all. It was emanating from the back seat of our refurbished '71 convertible! The light began to grow even brighter as I tapped at Ronald's shoulder. I could see him already looking in the rear view mirror and before I could speak, he had begun to slow the car and proceed over into the breakdown lane. He shut off the car and grabbed my hand, just as bewildered and confused as I was. The light morphed and grew larger taking on the shape of a person. It looked like … no it couldn't be … but it was … it was Ronald's father. And he had passed away some fifteen years ago.

Then he spoke, "This is your father, Ronald, and I have been here watching over you. I know things have been rough for you lately. I understand, but all is well. I have your back. I love you."

And he slowly disappeared. We looked at each other in disbelief, then a feeling of deep peace settled over us. Ronald turned the car around and headed back to our house. It was well after midnight and the lights were still on. I patted Ronald's back as we pulled up into our driveway.

NEST

"The birds are building a nest." The comic started his routine like this every night with this line in his thick Jewish accent. Most nights the show ended up going very well with lots of laughs, clapping, and often times a standing ovation at the end. Joe's confidence rose steadily and we were sure he would soon hit the big time, with appearances on Kimmel and a round of other talk shows and late night TV. And then, his own Vegas residency, just like Elvis had. He would *WOW* the whole world with his ingenious lines of humor mixed in with a few song and dance routines. And I, his agent, worked very hard to get him the many bookings on his calendar.

Usually, as I said, most every night went terrific, except for this one. This night was different and it would be one that would change his life forever. A heavy rain fell in the Catskills, making travel difficult and the audience turnout was slim. I was watching the show from the back as I regularly did; he was my favorite client. Anyway, there were maybe ten or eleven people sitting in the audience, if that. Joe began his routine and no one was laughing. He ad libbed, "What am I standing in here, is this a morgue or what?" thinking that could get a laugh.

But a man in the audience was angry; perhaps he had been cut off in traffic earlier, or was still suffering from a recent divorce or loss of a loved one. I don't know why, but the next thing I know, this guy starts yelling, and booing. Then he jumped up on the stage and began swinging at Joe. He hit him in the jaw and Joe went flying; he was knocked unconscious.

A young woman in the audience, who was sitting by herself, ran up on stage attending to Joe. She started rubbing his forehead and kissing him on the opposite cheek. I ran up behind her and heard her say, "You are going to be alright. You'll be fine." Joe opened his eyes and he was mesmerized, as he would later reveal to me, starring up into her wide, sparkling, blue and violet flecked eyes and enormous smile.

By now the bouncer had grabbed the guy and tossed him out. I pulled Joe up and made the announcement that the show was to be postponed. Then I took him back to his dressing room, and the woman followed. I didn't have the heart to tell her to go away, as Joe made it clear he had something to say to her. Against my better judgement I ushered her into the room and left them alone while I went out to the dining room for a grilled cheese. Tomorrow, I would be sure to contact him early and extract the details.

The next day I met Joe for breakfast and he filled me in on some of what happened after I left. Seems the two of them got on swimmingly. They sat on his couch and talked for hours. Had a lot in common even though she was twenty years his junior. He said he wanted to see where this would take him. "But what about your career, Joe?" I said. "You've been working for years now towards your dreams of getting on Fallon, Kimmel and Colbert."

"I know, that's the point. Years now. How many more years? I know I'm good, but it's brutal out there; it's dog-eat-dog. Something changed for me last night. I'm done with the sharks circling the tank. I want a real life, and I want to give this thing with Gina a real chance."

Needless to say, I couldn't convince Joe otherwise. I kept at him, but he wouldn't budge. That was it, and he wouldn't hear another word. So I cut him loose.

It's been 10 years now, and they're still happily married. They tied the knot just 6 months after that fateful night. I hear they have two kids, a girl and a boy, and they live out in the suburbs of New Jersey. Well, more power to them. I have other clients. And I'm doing fine.

LAST DAY AT THE NURSERY

They took their last lunch break together under the shade of the towering pecan trees. The nursery was shutting down, the owners were retiring. The water fountains were turned off and almost everything had been sold in the huge liquidation sale running the past three weeks.

Savanah pulled out her cheese, crackers and grapes from her purple nylon bag after settling into the rusted teal blue "beach chair" and asked Paulette what she was going to do next. "I have no idea," Paulette said shaking her head glumly, taking a bite of her peanut butter sandwich.

"Me neither," sighed Savanah. Golden leaves floated from the pecan trees, fluttering in the warm breeze of a sunny Fall day. "I'm going to miss this place. We sure had a lot of fun working here. It was so beautiful with all these trees and flowering plants."

"Yes," Paulette agreed. "I loved watering the rose bushes, so many colorful blooms and varieties. I especially liked that lavender one. Oh, and the orange too."

"Yea, and I enjoyed taking care of the geraniums, hydrangeas, pansies and chrysanthemums.

Oh well, what can we do … c'est la vie."

"Girls! Girls, can you come over here." The boss, Candy, was calling them from the shop that had housed all the fertilizers, plant food, rakes, shovels, gifts and garden decorations, including butterfly wheels, angel and gnome statues, welcome flags, flower door mats, souvenir coffee mugs and T-shirts. Savanah and Paulette walked over to meet her. "I decided I don't need you the rest of the afternoon so you can go home now. I have your last paycheck up front."

The girls collected their belongings, eyes brimming over with tears. Hugs were shared, farewells were said. The owner gifted Paulette with the yellow garden hose she had wanted, and Savanah got her dragonfly mailbox cover she coveted from the gift shop.

Paulette and Savanah solemnly shuffled to their cars. They stood talking with each other in the parking lot for a while. "Let's get together sometime," Savanah said. Paulette agreed, even though deep down she knew they never would. They traded phone numbers anyway and before they could get in their cars, the owner called out, "Wait a minute. Savanah, Paulette. Hold on." Candy came running out. I just got a call from my sister in California. She has an orchard and a nursery too, and she just told me she needs help. Several workers walked off the job and now she has no one to harvest the apples. She could use the help if you are willing to travel."

The girls looked at each other; Savanah was the first to speak. "I don't know Candy, it sounds like temporary work and it is a long way to travel. And where would we stay?"

"My sister has several cabins on the property for workers that come from a distance. You'd be welcome there. And it's not too far from Brier Mountain. There's lots of good hiking and there's a lake where you can kayak. The nearby town is cute with lots of shops and really good restaurants: a fantastic Italian one, another that has burgers to die for, and there's Chinese too."

"That sounds interesting, Candy," Paulette said. "Real good actually. And I don't have any plans right now. Got nothing going on....Yes, I'll take your sister up on her offer."

"Great! And what about you Savanah?"

"I have my family here. And the girls are in school. I can't take them out for a job so far away and temporary. I'll pass, but thanks anyway."

Paulette and Savanah hugged again. Paulette shook hands with Candy ready to start on a fresh course, travel a new road in what would actually turn out to be a most fortunate twist to her life.

FIVE DAY WRITING CHALLENGE

She signed up for the online writing challenge - 5 days 100 words only, each day a new topic. Exploring new ways to expand her skills, and maybe even win a prize, she was gung-ho ready to go.

The first day's theme: Origins - what happy childhood memory would someone have? So she wrote: Running down the hallway in my feet pajamas, must have been five, bursting into the living room on Christmas morning, my brother and sister not far behind. There it was, everything I asked for: big red wheels with the white swirl, handles to grip and turn, yellow seat surrounded in yellow round circle plastic. My Crazy Car. On the driveway when there was no snow - squeals of dizzy fun - forward, backward, spinning circles in the sunlight. The rumble of plastic to pavement brought years of fun. There's the old photo. Me, sitting in my Crazy Car, spinning in the sun....

Wow, that was fun. She entered her piece in the contest and now she was ready for Day 2... Leaving - write about a time when someone leaves to venture out on their own. Pen in hand she jotted this down: After all this time, they came to give support - helped me load up the U-haul with my belongings. I drove my car four hours to the city, following them. Then by myself after the goodbyes. New place and no job. To the market for groceries: stocked up on peanut butter. I drove home the next weekend to do my wash. And the next weekend too. So many people bustling, above ground subway rumbling, horns blaring, pushing and shoving - all this to follow a dream. To be an actress, the one standing on stage, applauded. I stand at the corner of my new street. The traffic light changes and the group crosses. I'm alone but not alone....

Another great writing session, she thought, and was looking forward to Day 3... Describe a beautiful moment. So she wrote: Outside open door golden leaved November trees and kids on squeaky swings - I hear them when we finish the song: his red guitar strumming fingers, my tambourine striking wrist, stamping red patent leather shoes onto cement. Vocalizing "So You Want To Be A Rock 'N' Roll Star." Mia, young teen in her black converse - dancing, waving; her brother Otis drops a tip in the red ribbon plastic jar. There's clapping; David says he loves it - simple music without bells and whistles. In wafts smokey smell of barbecue pulled pork and hamburger, cool fan blows on the back of my head, my hands are chilled....

Oh boy she was on a roll, really enjoying the writing challenge. Day 4 - write about a reunion with someone from the past. She wrote: It's six years since they had seen each other. She was eighteen now and flew to London with her parents: a graduation trip. That summer day a taxi drove them through the countryside, past rolling hills in misty green with sheep lazily grazing, to the cottage of her Japanese friend. Remembering that time when she was twelve and her friend taught her how to make origami, say Good Evening and count numbers in Japanese. Today Masako greeted her at the door in a striking royal blue sweater, her lips painted ruby. Come in.

They hugged. I'm making Roast beef with Yorkshire pudding....

Nice one, she thought. Finally it was the last day - Day 5. The theme was nature and spirit, wonder, magic and awe. So she wrote: 8 am train out of city; we're free. Cute room at Bed and Breakfast. We walk barefoot though beach and ocean breezes, springtime warm, to the supermarket for already cooked baked chicken, raw vegetables. I pack a bag for our sunset outing - Appetizers: cheese, crackers, topped off glasses to cheer. Watched the sun sink below the

horizon in oranges, pinks, yellows. Dark now, moonless, twinkling stars, crashing waves in the blackness, phantom grassy dunes behind us, lying back down on the woolen blanket, holding hands.... There's movement above, in the sky way up. A zig zag light, turning on a dime, ninety degree angle, forward, sideways, back, then racing off. It's not a plane. We grab our blanket and run.

Every day she entered her writing in the contest. She didn't win. Did she want to go on and try for publication ... or just write for her own fun and enjoyment?

JASMINE AND ROSES

The scent of jasmine and roses wafted high above the mountaintops and would soon descend upon the little village located on the northern side of the peninsula that jutted out to welcome the deep blue and turquoise sea. Shalimar was seated at the small round rough-wooden table in the little palm-thatched hut, busy knitting her grandfather an off-white woolen sweater for the cool nights soon to be upon them. She paused every so often to take a sip of her rose hip tea.

Shalimar lived with her parents and five brothers and sisters in the small community known for it's finely woven colorful blankets and soft fleece garments. Her grandparents lived not far from them, just down the narrow dirt road, lined with banana, coconut and palm trees.

Late in the afternoon, there was a knock on the door and Shalimar jumped. She was alone; everyone else in the family was out in the fields harvesting rice or down in the pasture tending the sheep and goats. The knocking persisted, getting louder by the second. Shalimar leapt up, her knitting needles and yarn toppling to the floor. "Who is it?" she called out timidly.

"I have a message for you," came the response. The voice sounded soft, gentle in nature.

Feeling a bit reassured, Shalimar put on her midnight blue cape and walked to the door, but not before first peering out the window a few yards away. She saw a man, tall with broad shoulders. He had light brown hair, a long beard, and was dressed in robes of gold and scarlet, giving him an air of royalty. In his hands he held a large, oval, sparkling emerald green box.

Intrigued, Shalimar, who just turned twenty-one three days before, wondered if one of the villager's relatives was giving her a belated birthday present. She had a wonderful birthday party, with most of the residents stopping by to celebrate the big day. But what was this glittering emerald box with a message to go along with it? This was starting to sound exciting. "Please come in and sit down," Shalimar held the door open for the gentleman and quietly closed it behind him.

The man walked regally over to the couch, sat down and immediately opened the dazzling box. He pulled out a long scroll of paper. "Before I begin, I'd like to say that we have been watching you quite closely. We have made our decision, and now you must make yours."

"What are you talking about?" Shalimar was confused. "Who is 'we'? And who are you?" This didn't seem like the nice present she'd begun to expect from someone in the settlement.

Without answering Shalimar's question, he continued, "I will first read to you what is on this scroll." And he began, "You, Shalimar Siegfried, are requested, of your own free will of course, to make a choice concerning you, your family and your communities' welfare. It will not be an easy one, and you will have a considerable amount of time to think this over."

Now, Shalimar was getting nervous. "Can I get you a cup of tea?" She needed a distraction. "No, that won't be necessary. May I go on?"

"Of course. Please." But that's not what she was really thinking. She wasn't at all sure if she wanted to hear something that sounded dire or worse.... On the other hand, she did want to do whatever she could to help her family and neighbors. She looked directly into the stranger's eyes. He stared back at her kindly, but intently. Her fingers began to quiver, and she felt numb. Then her whole body began to shake. A second later lightning flashed across the room. Shalimar could see and hear nothing; everything had turned white and silent. Only the strong, fervent fragrance of jasmine and roses wafted to her nose as she passed out and fell to the floor.

COLD FEET

The slow moving overhead fan spun fairly ineffective. Georgie brushed a strand of sticky hair from her forehead and took a big gulp of iced coffee, all but one of the cubes melted. From the speakers in the coffee shop came lyrics from a Madonna song: "...*Open your heart to me, I'll give you love if you turn the key.*" Anxiety echoed in her head and ricocheted down her body. She was thirty-three years old and what had she done? The last few day's events played across the movie screen of her mind. Her boyfriend of six months got a job in Vegas and he asked her to move there with him. Georgie had said yes, but Vegas was a long way from her hometown of Wooster, Ohio. Jeff was out in Vegas now starting his new job as a blackjack dealer and she was driving there after giving up her apartment, putting things in storage and packing her car with just the bare minimal. She had stopped at a coffee shop in Kansas and was now having second thoughts. Serious second thoughts. Hot as she was, Georgie was getting cold feet.

She picked up her cell and dialed Jeff's number. "Jeff ... it's Georgie. I was thinking ..." "What is it? Are you all right?"

"I'm fine. I'm in Topeka now, but ... I can't move to Vegas with you. I'm going back to Ohio. "What? Why?"

"I just can't that's all."

"What are you talking about? Baby, come on ... I love you."

"You think you do now, but I'm a lot older than you. What happens when I turn fifty? I can't do it Jeff. I have to break this off now. Before it goes any further." After she said that, she hung up. She didn't want to be talked out of it. Georgie put her head in her hands.... Maybe she was being too hasty. Maybe she *should* give it a chance. It she didn't at least try with Jeff, she'd never know. Georgie thought about picking up the phone again, telling him she changed her mind. But then she thought of the children she always wanted and how her clock was ticking. As much as Jeff said he wanted kids too, she knew he wasn't ready. Georgie took another sip of her iced coffee. What to do? Maybe she could change Jeff's mind and convince him to have kids sooner than later. She picked up a Cosmopolitan magazine lying on the table near her and flipped through the pages. All those pretty girls. All those pretty girls in big cities, like Vegas. Georgie was thinking of the wrinkle lines that were starting to appear more prominent under her eyes and at the corners of her mouth. And she had put on a few pounds since high school. Let's face it, she wasn't so young and beautiful anymore. Georgie remembered back in high school when many a boy came calling for her, though there was only one she really liked and cared for. And times had changed; after college she took a waitressing job to pay the bills and never left. Until now, when it seemed exciting to move to Vegas with her boyfriend. Except she couldn't do it … or could she. Still wracked with confusion, Georgie paid her bill and was about to head to the ladies room when someone came up behind her.

"Georgie, is that you?" The voice sounded so familiar. She whirled around and gasped. There was her high school sweetheart, the one she really wanted, the only one she cared for. But it all fell apart when he went to college out of state, across the country, and they lost touch.

"What are you doing here?"

"I live in Topeka, got a job right out of college. I can't believe I'm seeing you. I missed you." As he took her hands in his, Georgie glanced down. There was no wedding ring on his finger.

CHRISTMAS CHOIR

I sat at my desk listening to the voice of the principal read the morning announcements over the loud speaker. "After classes today, all choir members are to report to the gym for the first rehearsal of the Christmas concert." I felt sick. I had just managed to squeak by at the audition and make it into the choir, though I don't know how. My voice wasn't right I thought, but either there weren't enough people trying out, or the director saw something in me, though I can't figure out what. I had always wanted to sing, but at home I was ridiculed by my family. My cousin even said, "Wow, you really can't sing," when I had practiced and put all my efforts into my greatest rendition of "Crazy," the song sung and made famous by Patsy Cline. Anyway, it took a lot of nerve for me to try out for the choir, but now that I got in I felt worse. What if I couldn't cut it and they dropped me, like they did to Lucy Black last year. She never lived it down with all the ribbing she got from our classmates. She finally switched schools, didn't come back to Washington Middle School this year.

All day long I was wracked with nerves. I barely heard what my teachers were teaching. In English class, Mr. Dobbs asked me if I knew what a conjunctive adverb was. He had to call my name again before I got that he was talking to me, and then I had to say I didn't hear the question. And of course I didn't know the answer either. Then in science class, I almost poured the wrong ingredient into the photosynthesis solution, but Alex stopped me in time. He said I could have caused an explosion…. It's just that I was so worried; I really wanted to do well in the choir, show my parents and everyone else that I could sing.

Finally the bell rang at 2:20 and school was out. I went to my locker and grabbed all the books I needed for homework that night. Then I slowly made my way to the gym and sat on the bleachers with the other nineteen members who were already there before me. Mr. Kostyla was passing out the song list and when he came to me, he looked me in the eye while saying to everyone, "No one is allowed to be late to rehearsal, from now on. I expect everyone to be here on time." I knew he was talking about me; already I was getting off to a bad start. I looked at the song list and saw we would be singing *Oh Come All Ye Faithful, Winter Wonderland,* and *Let It Snow* among others.

"Okay, let's start with *Oh Come* Ye *Faithful"* our music instructor said. "Everyone now, here we go." He tapped on the podium, "And a one, and a two, three, and four..."

I opened my mouth, "Oh come all ye ..." I sang and stopped. What came out of my mouth was the sound of a high pitched squeal. Yikes. Everyone heard it and stopped in their tracks.

"Is anything wrong, Miss Parker?" Mr. Kostyla asked.

"No, I ... ah ..." My throat was dry and that's all I could stammer out. We tried again. I squawked. Boy I was really messing up. I couldn't see me being invited to come back for another day of rehearsal. Flashes of all the times I was ridiculed raced through my head, like a sad movie where the heroine dies in the end, humiliated and defeated.... Humph. Well this time it wouldn't be me! I would believe I could do it! I would have faith in myself, faith - like in the song.

"Okay one more time. Everyone ... and a one ... I pulled back my shoulders, stood tall, opened my mouth and let it rip. I sang louder than everyone else, and right on key. My voice rose, fell, hit all the notes. One by one everyone stopped singing and let me finish the song alone, giving me rousing applause when I was done. And Mr. Kostyla said, "Congratulations!"

PLANET BLUE, BLUE PLANET

Planet blue, blue planet - These were the words printed on a poster tacked to a telephone pole in downtown Cleveland. People were curious when they passed by, but most continued on, puzzled but concluding it was just an advertisement for the local environmental lobbyists.

However, some were intrigued and wanted to know more. I was one of those who wanted to find out more. And it wasn't just the words, planet blue, blue planet that had me curious. It was the tagline below which added to the mystery: *Call this number for a chance to win the grand prize, to be named later.* So I, having been long-time tired of my ho-hum humdrum life, decided to 'take the bait,' as they say.

When I got back to my meagerly-furnished, run-down apartment, I sat on the old ripped- leather couch and called the number. At first it was exactly as I expected. "Hello, planet blue, blue planet," came the operator's voice.

"Hello I replied, "I saw your poster with the number to call." "Yes, I was expecting you."

"Me?'

"Yes, you. But first I have to ask you a few questions. And if you pass, I have something I need you to do before I can submit your name in the grand prize drawing."

"Okay?" I was starting to wonder about all of this. It sounded odd, but I said she could go on and proceed with the questions. First she asked me basic ones like name and age range, and if I was in good physical health. Then the questions became more in depth: Did I like living where I was and why, and would I ever like to go anywhere else, and where. I gave her my answers including letting her know I was bored and would be glad to go somewhere else but I didn't have the money.

"Great, you passed. Congratulations!" she voiced through the receiver. "And now I need you to do something…. Go down to your local market on Seventh Street and ask for Randy. He will give you further instructions."

After we hung up, I got nervous. I wasn't sure where this was leading, but then again she seemed seriously happy that I passed some kind of test. I hemmed and hawed a little, but then decided I would go through with her request. I knew just the market she was talking about; it was on the corner at the end of my street, and I had been there many a time. Though I never knew anyone by the name of Randy who worked there. I grabbed my umbrella and raincoat as it had begun to rain since late afternoon and headed for the store. The rain looked sparkling pretty as it fell below the streetlights and the reflections it made in the puddles seemed otherworldly.

I opened the door to the market; bells chimed against the glass. A girl with auburn hair walked up to me and asked if I was Penny. I said yes.

"We've been expecting you," she said, using almost the same words the operator stated over the phone. "Follow me to the back room, please."

Somehow I felt safe enough and followed her through the swinging black double doors. It was dark and I couldn't see a thing. I started to panic. Suddenly all the lights went on and a whole group of people yelled, *Surprise*! They began to clap and cheer. Randy stepped forward, "You're the winner!" And he handed me a ticket for one free ride on the International Space Station circling *Planet Blue, Blue Planet* - Earth! I could not have been any happier.

TREE

Jim and I were sitting at the kitchen counter having fried eggs and bacon when Sherrie, our neighbor, called. Jim picked up the phone to hear her screech, "Jim, can you come over! A big branch from the pine in front of the house fell on the roof, and when I went into the dining room this morning, there was a mess of water on the floor. There's a huge hole in the roof!"

"Of course. That was quite a storm last night. The wind was really whipping and the rain pelted our windows for hours. Don't worry, I'll be right over."

My husband made his living as a handyman and always had a line of customers waiting for his services. He was good at his work and I knew he could handle whatever came his way. He grabbed his jacket and exited the front door. "I'll be back in time for lunch."

"Okay, I'll have the potato salad with scallions ready for our hot dogs and sauerkraut."

Lying in the hospital bed that evening with his head fully bandaged, Jim told me his side of the story and all that happened after he left. When he got to Sherrie's, the problem was worse than he expected. Broken twigs, pine needles, mud and water covered the linoleum floor, and the gaping hole in the ceiling revealed the massive branch lying above. "I'll start by cleaning up the floor and then get to removing the branch from the roof," he told her. He'd just started with a broom and shovel, when there was a loud cracking sound. As he looked up the rest of the ceiling came crashing down upon him, a heavy chunk of plaster knocking him unconscious.

There was a lot of blood and Sherrie immediately called 911. She ran to get me and we both rode in the ambulance with Jim. I was a wreck and kept talking to him, trying to get him to wake up, but he remained unconscious all the way to the hospital where he was wheeled directly into surgery. I paced the floors wringing my hands, both Sherrie and I often in tears. I was so worried he'd die like my aunt who was in a coma for years until they eventually had to pull the plug.

Finally Jim was out of surgery and the doctor came to tell us that he'd be okay. A severe concussion only, and skin wounds. The tests showed no serious brain injury, thank God.

Sherrie left for home and I stayed with Jim through the night, never more relieved and in love with him, so thankful for his survival and imminent well being. Everyone at the hospital was very nice and treated us with kindness and compassion. I told Jim I was going to buy the staff a monstrous box of homemade chocolates that this shop downtown makes. So creamy and delicious, including my favorites - orange cream, raspberry cream, lemon and hazelnut.

Two days later Jim went home and we sat at our kitchen counter again, this time realizing, *Hey, life's too short.* What else would we want to do? How could we live life a little more fully? I fixed a big plate of maple pecan pancakes, and got out a piece of paper to write a bucket list.

"I don't know if I can think of anything, Honey ... and besides that, my customers need me." "Yes, they do Jim, but if you don't do what you'd like to now, who knows, you may never get the chance," I countered. "What about traveling together to Europe ... or the two of us making beautiful music together, you singing with your guitar and me on tambourine. We could join the music circuit and play for people around the country. Or maybe go back to school and learn a new subject or skill. You once thought about becoming an architect. And I always wanted to be an artist, painting big canvas' in acrylics. We could still do these things. It's not too late."

"Maybe you're right. And if it wasn't for this tree that fell on Sherrie's roof, I never would have thought to do or try anything different. Thanks, Love. Yes, new things are on the way!

MONOLOGUE

Hi, my name is Doris Fitsimons, and for today's audition I'll be doing a monologue from ... What? ... You want me to talk about what I see in that picture you have hanging up, instead of reciting my monologue? ... Okay, well then ... I see nature: trees, rocks, ferns, pink flowers, blue sky; there's a dirt path, birds flying, a light in the distance. It looks like the sun. Hmmm.

Yes, I like nature.... Reminds me of when I used to go out in it when I was a kid. My Uncle Griswold would take me and my two brothers for hikes when he wasn't working at his jewelry business. Mostly we went in the summertime, but sometimes in winter too. Anyway, I guess what I remember most about those hikes were all the times my uncle had to get me and my brothers out of a jam. Like the time when Aron went running across a frozen lake in December. Only it wasn't completely frozen and he fell through. Oh my God, I started screaming and Uncle Griswold, cool as a cucumber, maneuvered himself onto the ice, spread his body flat and grabbed Aron's hand - it was still waving and sticking above the water. Uncle pulled him to safety, but boy that was a close one. Aron caught a cold after that, but he was fine. Yikes!

Oh, then there was this other time when I took us on a different path from the one we usually went on and we all came face to face with a bear. Well not really face to face; the bear was one hundred yards ... or maybe it was two hundred yards away. But we were still shaking in our boots. My uncle told us to back away quietly, slowly and quietly, slowly ... and whew, we were lucky, the bear didn't come after us - probably because there were no young to protect. That was really scary. We could have been goners.

Ahh ... um ... okay, then once, and it was the summer I got out of middle school ... I remember because I just had my first crush on a boy. His name was Albert and I was heartbroken because he told me his father got transferred and they were moving to Arkansas.

Anyway, I was on this hike; my head was down, all bummed out, cursing my fate. I was last in line and David was leading our little troop. He had run up ahead of us and found a deserted campsite. By the time we caught up to him, we saw him with a big stick, poking and stirring at the fire site.

Flames started shooting up, big spitting, licking-at-you kind of flames. Seems the campers didn't bother to make sure everything was put out. "Fire!" David yelled. Alright that was obvious, but then I started to panic. Even though I'd lost my true love, I didn't want to die out there. What if the whole forest went up in flames? My whole body froze and I couldn't move until Uncle Griswold yelled, "Grab all the water bottles and douse it!" My brothers and I 'snapped to' and we dumped the water. Then Uncle Griswold took off his jacket and smothered the rest of the fire with it. Smoke rose, the fire was out, Uncle's jacket was a blackened char, and we all cheered … and did some high-five's and little dances too around the extinguished campfire.

Oh! Oh! I remember another time when … What? … You want me to stop now? … Aww, okay then…. Well, thank you, thank you. I hope you enjoyed this audition and I hope I get this job…. I can't see you out there with all these lights…. Did I say my name was Deborah? I mean Doris. Doris Fitsimons. And here's an extra head shot for you. Where are those stairs?

WHY DID ROSE PICK UP THE STICKS

Silvia was creating a new nature video that she planned to edit and post on YouTube in a couple of days. Today she pulled out her drone from the garage, having decided that some aerial shots would really be super, seeing that the mountain trees were in full fiery array with Fall colors. The combination of the reds, oranges and yellows would be beautifully juxtaposed with each other. Silvia started the drone and sent it high into the sunlit sky, manning the control switches from her backyard below. She was excited, thinking this would be her best video yet.

Silvia was just out of high school and hoped to become a videographer or a movie director one day. She was thinking of entering college the following year as she needed the extra time to save up money for tuition. She also hoped to apply for a scholarship and present samples of her work for consideration of acceptance into the prestigious New York Film Academy.

This nature project was her most recent attempt at creating a 'knock 'em dead' film.

Everything was going well until a stiff wind picked up. It came on surprisingly fast and furious. Before Silvia could get the drone back, it was caught up in a strong gust and went tumbling and whirling away, smashing into a cliff of white rock and falling down somewhere amongst the trees far up on the mountainside. Silvia was devastated since this piece of equipment had cost her a lot of money. She had to get it back and see if there was some way to repair it, or if not, maybe she could salvage some of the pictures that it had already captured. Silvia grabbed her backpack and a couple of water bottles and set off in the direction of where it fell. She wove her way through the woods, maneuvering around rocks, stepping over brush, making her way up a jagged hill. This area of the mountain was obscure and unmarked; a place that she, and probably no one else had ever hiked before. At the top of the hill there was a little clearing where she could see the drone sticking up from a bed of pine needles and fallen leaves. Feeling lucky that she was able to find it, Silvia ran over and picked up the damaged drone, tucking it gently into her backpack. Then she sat on a large, flat rock and drank from her water bottle. Silvia glanced to her right and noticed what appeared to be a solitary stone chimney standing amongst some tall ferns and bushes. Curious, she walked over to enter the remnants of a burned out old house. As she meandered around the structure, wondering who could have lived there and lost their home, she stopped short of almost stepping on a small structure made of sticks. Popsicle sticks. Silvia knelt down and picked up a popsicle stick house. The wood was worn; it looked like it had been there awhile, but it was still in relatively good shape. There were doors, and windows with small pink curtains pasted on, and inside there was miniature furniture glued to the floor. Silvia turned the house around and over and saw a small plastic bag attached to the bottom of the house. There was a note inside and Silvia pulled it out to read the words: I am Rose and I picked up these sticks to make this little house. It's a collectable!

Silvia was enamored with this miniature popsicle house. However, she couldn't help but wonder why Rose would bother to pick up sticks to make a nice little house and then leave her creation in the middle of a big abandoned burned out house high up in the mountain woods, where no one was even likely to travel. Then she got an idea. She would use this popsicle stick house in her film, create a whole story and backstory around it. This film would be the winning straw, or 'stick' to help get her into college with a top-level, full scholarship.

CARVED FACES

An old man sat in an art shop wearing a canvas cap pasted with sea shells. He was carving a piece of wood and I stopped to ask what he was making. "I'm finishing work on a *funny face*," he replied pointing to a wall where a large number of carved faces hung. I looked over and was mesmerized by the handiwork. In all shapes and sizes were fascinating and captivating creations of art. Faces that wore smiles, frowns, males, females, some appeared ferocious, and some looked just plain crazy. I thanked the artist and left, the many images locked into my mind.

That evening, sitting by the fireplace and looking at YouTube on my laptop, I found an interesting video by *The Parlotones - It's Magic*. I was particularly intrigued by the first verse: *Autumn melts down on the ground it colors, The streets are filled with art and the trees the artists, It's magic, it's magic, I dream of the future, my sisters and my brothers, No more war, just love for one another.* And the video's visual art was amazing with paper trees rising from the ground, a paper star tumbling up to the heavens, a smiling crescent moon, and paper birds flying.

After a day filled with new pictures spinning in my head, I extinguished the fire in the fire place, crawled up to the second floor and soon fell fast fell asleep. That's when I had the dream.

One of the mahogany wood-sculptured faces from the art store came to life, took on a bodily form and invited me to go on an adventure. She was sitting on the back of one of the big paper birds from the video and told me to hop on. Well I wasn't one to turn down a chance for some new excitement, even in my dreams, so I immediately said yes. I swung my leg up and sat behind her. We soared up through the roof of my house, rising high into the air, way above planet earth. I could see the continents, the oceans, clouds, sun shining on part of the earth and darkness on the other. We turned and headed off toward the stars, and then beyond the stars and past our swirling galaxy. We traveled far, in the blink of an eye almost, to another universe. I could see many planets there, but one dazzled and glowed brighter than the rest - and that was the one this carved lady took us to. We gently landed in a field surrounded by tall green pines. There was a cool breeze blowing and a sun shone warmly over us. Overall, there seemed to be an amazing likeness to our own planet earth in the way this planet looked. Except something felt different.

There was a layer of calmness and serenity that blanketed this planet. I could hear soothing sweet sounds of music floating in the air. As we walked down a path lined with flowers I began to notice a few more differences. All the colors were more vibrant, alive and bright - the pinks more glowing pink, the purples more rich, more purple than I'd ever seen. I looked up and saw flying creatures soaring in a rapturous display of freedom and delight. The *Carved Woman,* who hadn't said a word to me, but was communicating to me with her thoughts, motioned for me to sit down by this crystal azure lake we were approaching. Out of thin air she pulled a large woven picnic basket and a royal blue blanket. We sat comfortably and she pulled out the most scrumptious goodies from the basket: sweet fruits, buttered rolls, fine cheeses and chocolate strawberry croissants.We washed the refreshments down with clear spring water, and I asked her questions on all kinds of subjects. She answered every question plus talked some more about herself and her planet - the way all beings came together with a deep desire to get along and live in peace.

Time passed, more or less, and she said we had to go back. With a whoosh I was back in my bedroom; we hugged and I waved goodbye to the *Carved Woman* and big bird.

I awoke refreshed and excited for finding that video and those carved faces in the art shop.

DISENCHANTED

I stood there motionless, disenchanted by the whole spectacle.

My husband, Jerry, had been involved in the space program for nearly twenty years. Most of that time he spent training to be an astronaut. It was his dream since he was a child and he could not let go of it. And I have to say that his goals had taken a toll on our marriage. He was away a lot of the time and in some of those years we often moved around, uprooted from our home, family and friends. The kids had to leave school and start all over several times due to his ongoing training in different areas of the country. When he was in class and pursuing new fields of study, taking various tests, we didn't see him for days on end and I was left to raise the kids alone. I might add that they didn't turn out so bad either. Jannie is an oncologist and Mark is in banking. I'm very proud of them. Anyway, the higher-ups kept promising Jerry flight and even though he often failed their rigorous physically demanding tests, they still kept telling him, "One day you'll fly, my boy, one day you'll fly." So day and night, as I said, he was busy, busy... busy.

Anyway, after two decades, they finally gave my husband the green light on a trip to Mars.

Oh he was excited alright, to say the least. He'd be dancing around the house, singing some John Denver flight songs, like *Looking For Space* and *Fly Away,* totally ignoring the *Flying For Me* song. I didn't forget the Challenger tragedy and I had been beset with worry since I got the news of his upcoming flight. He was the love of my life, even though he'd driven me crazy with his long absences. And now going to Mars, no less. He'd be gone forever, if he even made it back.

I started thinking about all the good times we had together, sparse as they were. The time he took me to see the Jimmy Buffett concert down in Pasadena, and the Jimmy Buffett concert in Key

Largo and then there was Jones Beach in New York, another great time in Phoenix, Arizona and again in Vegas. Ok, I admit it, we were and still are Parrotheads. And those tailgate parties were something else. We stopped going to tailgates once the kids came along, but we still had just as much fun showing up in time for the concert, glad to hear the great, upbeat music.

Anyway, back to what I was talking about. This trip to Mars was an effort to discover more information about previous life on the planet. He and seven others would set up camp underground and would traverse the planet above ground ensconced in heavy cumbersome spacesuits to discover evidence of life or previous life. They would take samples, shoot in-depth photographs and see if it was possible to survive there now, in hopes that people of earth might be able to live there one day in the future.

That morning dawned sunny as we said our tearful goodbyes. The kids were crying too, and we all drove to Cape Canaveral together, still in and out of tears. We had coffee and English muffins in the NASA cafeteria before Jerry said it was time for him to get ready.

I guess I was all cried out, and now I just felt numb. An hour later I stood in the stands several hundred kilometers from the launch pad. The countdown had begun. I wondered how our life might have been different if my husband had picked a different path, a different occupation. I wondered if I might have pursued a different path and had not even married him at all.

There was a blast of power, force and noise. There were swirling grey clouds and flames of orange as the rocket shot up slow at first, gaining speed, taking my husband up and out of our atmosphere, away from me and this earth. My husband's dream came true and I just stood there with my kids next to me, motionless and disenchanted by the whole spectacle.

MISS KITTY'S

Two days before spring and snow and freezing temperatures met us head on. We were traveling on Interstate 40 and had just made it to the little town before the highways were closed. Luckily there were plenty of rooms available at this cute little country inn.

Of course we were hungry, so after hauling our suitcases up to our second floor balcony room and taking a few minutes to freshen up, we headed down to Miss Kitty's for some good old fashioned ribs, baked beans and cornbread. The food was delicious, the lights were low just the way we liked them, and the ambience was great too. There was a piano player sitting in the corner playing standards, contemporary folk rock tunes and taking requests. We relaxed, enjoyed our conversation and forgot all about the snow and how we almost skidded off the road into a big ditch. There had been a huge tractor trailer in front of us and the driver jacked on his breaks. We swerved and skidded to avoid him and almost went off the side of the road to either be killed or at the very least stranded in a pile of heavy snow deep down in a ditch. Yes, we were very glad our lives weren't lost, happy to still be 'alive and kicking.'

The candle on our table was still going strong and we were just finishing our coffee and apple crumb pie when someone two tables over requested *On The Road*, the smash hit by Tim Young that was taking the country by storm. Most people knew the lines already, so practically everyone in the restaurant was singing along. Someone even got up from their table and did a few spins around the room. Actually more than a few people took to the dance floor.

When the piano player finished the song, everyone clapped and that's when I got up. I couldn't help myself. I dinged on my water glass, "Everyone, you've been so gracious in your love and support of Tim Young's song, that I'd like to take this time to present you with a little surprise." Tim took off his wig and dark glasses, gave me an amusing smile and stood up. "Tim Young, everybody!" I boomed out to the crowded restaurant.

For a moment the room went quiet. People couldn't believe it was actually him standing there. Then a flashbulb went off from someone's iPhone. More flashes from phones, and then someone came up to our table asking for an autograph. A line formed and everyone wanted Tim's autograph. He was signing napkins, paper table placemats, men's baseball caps, women's sweatshirts, postcards and notepads.

I could tell Tim enjoyed it all, especially because him being there was such a surprise to everyone. He kindly posed for more pictures and signed more autographs, taking time to have a little chat with each person.

Well, it was getting late and I could see Tim was getting tired. We politely excused ourselves as Tim signed the last autograph for the manager of Miss Kitty's, who said dinner was on the house. "Thanks, everyone," I said to the remaining patrons and we quietly left the restaurant and climbed the stairs to our room for what we hoped would be a comfy night's sleep. But not before we had a last real good laugh.

"Did you see the looks on their faces when you took off that curly blond wig and glasses?" "Yes, I did," Tim smiled. "They had no idea." We broke down into laughter, slapping our knees as we rolled into bed and snuggled under the covers, soon to fall fast asleep in each other's arms.

GIRL ON THE TRAIN

The girl on the train sat quietly contemplating her past. Too many sad memories, she thought, so she turned her attention outside the window. In the distance, tall mountains jutted upward to meet the azure sky, while low feathery white clouds circled the mountain's majestic peaks. The flat prairie beside her stretched for miles in all directions, it's golden grasses waved peacefully in the summer's breeze.

The girl gazed mindlessly at the tranquil scene for several minutes, then looked over at the empty chair beside her. She was missing that certain someone, the one that made all her days seem brighter. Now she was heading back East, alone, to pick up some of the pieces she thought she had left behind. She wasn't looking forward to being by the ocean again. Something about the sea and what it was able to do scared her. But her family's house needed to be sold and she was the one left in charge. The house was situated a mile from the beach, and while most people she knew loved being by the water, for some reason she dreaded her infrequent stays there. The girl looked out the train's window again and was surprised to see a lone buffalo up ahead and maybe a mile yonder. It appeared like it was charging toward her, fast approaching the train with mounds and mounds of dust rising in puffs around it, like smoke from a heavy wash of rain on dry desert-packed earth. For a moment the girl panicked, but then remembered she was sitting safely inside this heavyweight steel-clad casing. The creature continued it's forceful charge, relentless, seemingly oblivious to the moving steel block in front of it. A train attendant was passing down the isle making announcements of some sort, but all the girl could do was stare, frozen, out the window at the racing buffalo getting closer and closer to her and the train, until it was almost upon them. She turned to shout *Help* to the attendant, but no sound ushered from her lips. The girl looked back outside again, just as the buffalo leapt high, ready to crash into the window beside her. She expected the shattering of glass, but in that instant the animal froze in mid

112

air, motionless, front legs outstretched, nostrils flared and steaming, eyes glazed over, startled and bewildered.

The girl was just as mystified. What was happening, and why didn't the buffalo hit the train and shatter the glass? Partly relieved that she was out of danger, and partly worried that she might be going crazy, especially since none of the other passengers even noticed this scenario, the girl leaned back in her chair and closed her eyes, breathing deep. Then it came to her: she must be dreaming. She was having a lucid dream, fully aware of the vision that unfolded in front of her. She opened her eyes and now she saw a book lying on the seat beside her. She glanced over to read the title: *The Fall of Atlantis: Shattering of an Early Civilization.* And her eyes began to well up and the tears began to fall, dripping until she could barely hold back the sobs....

The flame of the candle flickered, casting shadows over the aged woman's face. Her soft blue eyes peered intently into the enormous crystal ball on the table in front of her. A feeling of sadness passed through her frail body as she pulled back from the vision of the girl on the train. For several minutes, the old woman wrung her hands together, sinews tense, then took two sips of her wildberry elixer. She smoothed back her greying hair, then rose from her chair, and walked over to open the door, letting in the ocean breeze. She looked out to sea, it's gentle waves lapping at the shore in front of her. The old woman shivered and wrapped the golden silk ties of her purple Atlantean robe more tightly around her waist as tears gathered and fell to the floor below.

I WANT TO DANCE

I want to dance like Charlotte did in her kitchen last night. Looking beautiful with her long blond hair, wearing her short, black velvet party dress with a matching black beret, and a garnet and diamond bracelet, she kicked off her silver patent leather heels and twirled to the music on the radio: *Helen Reddy - I Am Woman, Starship - Nothing's Gonna Stop Us Now, Patrick Hernandez - Born To Be Alive.* I sat on the little stool in the corner, too shy to join in.

Charlotte is my best friend. We met in high school when her family moved to our little town of Deerfield River. We were in a lot of the same classes together and we spent many a summer's day swimming and kayaking up and down the river. And nights camping out on its banks.

After high school our lives went separate ways - Charlotte went to the *Paris College of Art* while I stayed home and got a job cleaning rooms at the local hotel. My family didn't have the money to send me to college; that's just the way things were and I accepted it - for a while. That first year out of high school, Charlotte and I spent quite a bit of time chatting on the phone, but later calls between us became infrequent. I still considered Charlotte to be my best friend though.

When Charlotte finished her art studies, she traveled around the world painting these unique modern art canvas' from her experiences staying in quaint European hamlets, Asian villages and oceanside resorts. Now her paintings hang in several notable museums including MOMA.

Anyway, two days ago I got a call from Charlotte. She was back in town and wanted to get together. She gave me the address of the new home she recently purchased on the outskirts of town and told me to arrive at seven-thirty. Although I was tired from the long shift washing sheets, scrubbing bathrooms, mopping floors and vacuuming carpets, I looked forward to the visit. I was happy for her; I just felt a little sad about my lot. I couldn't help it. My life felt hard, and her's seemed so easy and nice. I stopped by my apartment to change into my new black jeans and emerald green woolen sweater and arrived on time. She made a great dinner for us: baked fillet of sole, orange glazed carrots, a mixed green salad and peach pie for desert. We caught up on all the little details that went on in our lives, though I didn't have that much to report. But Charlotte had some amazing stories to share on all her travels. And then she put on the radio and danced around the kitchen. I sat in the corner, an even deeper sadness washing over me.

The next day was Sunday and I got up early to take a hike on a trail down by the river. The sun was rising and the way it sparkled on the river was beautiful. I could hear the rushing water as it cascaded over rocks, weaving it's way downstream to some faraway place. Leaves crunched under my feet and a couple of cardinals flew by and landed in the tree up ahead of me.

Everything around me looked so beautiful. I thought on all that transpired the night before and suddenly I felt inspired. I wanted to dance like Charlotte did in her kitchen. Right here, right now. I took off my hiking boots and socks and started twirling, skipping, swinging and hopping to a song playing in my head. I danced fast with carefree abandon on the hard, cold dusty surface of the earth. Some hikers passed me by, wearing their parkas, scarfs, hats and mittens. It was thirty-eight degrees but I didn't care. I was oblivious to the people and the temperature. In that moment I felt like Charlotte - free, rich, the world at my feet. And then, in a moment of clarity, I knew that things would be different for me. I didn't know how, or when or where, but somehow in some way my life was definitely going to change. Dancing in my bare feet in the cold on that sunny Sunday morning I was absolutely positively sure my life was going to get better.

COFFEE SHOP TALK - TALES FROM THE 1940'S **

Turning my car into the parking lot of the coffee shop as rain splashed against the widows, I checked to see if my parents had arrived first and they had - their car was parked near the entrance. I grabbed my umbrella and stepped into the early summer shower, breathing in the fragrant country air and noticing the big pink roses in full bloom growing around the shop's perimeter. No bus fumes to breathe here, and no lack of greenery either.

Anyway, Dad called me earlier, said it was time for a get-together, and since I wasn't doing anything in particular that day, I said I'd meet them at two. I did some laundry and finished the last slice of watermelon before heading onto the freeway for the one hour drive it took me to get from my apartment in the city to the bakery shop in my old hometown.

Mom and Dad were already at the counter ordering their coffees - Dad's regular and Mom's decaf - when I stepped up to join them. "What'll you have?" Dad asked me. "I'm buying."

"A latte ... and a chocolate muffin. Thanks."

Mom and Dad added cinnamon muffins to the order and we found a quiet table in the corner by the window. Rain ran down the glass in intricate streams and outside people were dodging puddles and maneuvering umbrellas as they came and went from the cozy shop.

"How's things?" Mom asked me.

"Pretty much the same. Nothing new with me. How about you guys?"

"Just the usual," Dad said. "But you know, I was thinking about the old days … when I grew up in the 40's, and how everything has changed. I bet you have no idea."

"Not exactly." Some of his stories I'd heard, not all, but I didn't mind hearing them again. "Well here's one for you. When I was a boy scout, our troop master John was an organizer for the *Natick Old Timer's Jamboree*. The people in our town would put together a day long festival of games and refreshments for everyone. We had chowder and clam cakes, followed by a New England clambake - with clams, potatoes, and corn on the cob.

One year John was in charge of the games. We had sack races, three legged races, swimming races in Gorman's Pond, a greased pole climb and a greased pig chase. The greased pig chase was the most exciting part of the day because of the challenge to catch that pig. My brother Pat grabbed a leg but it slipped out of his hands. My friend Antonio got the tail and out from his fingers the tail oozed like melted butter. A few more lunges from Giovanni, Emilio, Mario and Dante and there were bodies everywhere falling to the ground, one on top of another, all scrambling to get up, all hoping to get a winning grip. It was not to be. The pig escaped and ran down the hill and into the woods. We found it four days later, with all the grease rubbed off.

Our scout master really cared about us kids and wanted us to enjoy ourselves. Times were tough back then with the war and all, and John wanted to make sure we were well cared for. He was one of our greatest heroes."

"Wow, that's a great story, Dad. I didn't know all the details behind the greased pig chase." "Glad you liked it. Next time I'll tell you another. And maybe your mother will tell you the story of how she had her own cow - a cow, Beverly, named after her."

Mom smiled and said she would tell the story. It was getting late and I had to get back. Tomorrow's work day was looming. We hugged and I got back in my car, waving to them through the rain stained windows as I turned out and headed for the interstate.

FEROCIOUS

The wind was ferocious; it had picked up speed to gale force and now the small fishing boat was in imminent danger. The crew of four cast off just before sunrise to reel in their lobster pots floating eight miles off the coast of Nova Scotia. They hoped for a big take, and yes, they were aware of a potential storm brewing, but thought they could make it back well before it hit.

The skies were mostly clear with a few wisps of pink and orange clouds rising high above the horizon as they left the dock and motored out northeast toward the many traps they'd set several days earlier. When they arrived at their destination and pulled up the pots, all were pleased to see many lobsters floating in the cages. They threw the females back into the sea and were still left with a considerable catch.

When they finished storing the lobsters in the large water-filled containers, they took a break, and that's when they noticed the dark menacing clouds gathering nearby. It seemed nature was following a different plan and the upset of wind and sea would be occurring much earlier than expected. They shifted the boat into high gear and began the trip back to shore. But the water quickly began to rise and crash against the sides of the vessel. It rocked violently and was brutally tossed about, like a rag doll thrown up against a crumbling wall by a tormented child.

Wave after wave jumped the sides of the boat, and the crew rapidly bailed out buckets of the water. Lightning and thunder flashed and cracked, and the wind screamed in their ears. Everyone was fast losing hope at their chances of survival. One man slipped and nearly fell overboard.

Then the youngest man in the group got down on his hands and knees to pray; he saw no other way out. He had a wife and family to care for, and didn't see them living securely and happily without him. "Please," he petitioned, as loud as he could muster, "please let us all live!" He hoped for a miracle and he kept on praying, while the other three men continued to rush about, frantically bailing water and attempting to keep the boat upright, sure they were going down.

A minute later lightning struck the tall mast and fire raced down the pole, igniting the rest of their vessel. All four men dived overboard, grabbing a life vest as they leapt, allowing them to stay afloat in the rocky and tumultuous sea. Hours passed and eventually the wind died down and the storm clouds dissipated. All the men were still alive, but separated from each other by miles.

Family members back home were extremely worried, and having put out a call to the Coast Guard, waited as patiently as they could for any word on their loved ones survival. At first the Coast Guard was hard pressed to find any signs to the men's whereabouts. They searched the ocean for two days, and due to their ongoing diligence, on the third day each of the men had been located and all returned safely to shore.

The men were severely dehydrated, and weak from lack of food. The families of the four nursed them back to health after they were released from the hospital. A few weeks passed before each of the fishermen was feeling back to normal. During their recuperation, everyone took stock of their lives and came to clear and confident decisions.Three of the men decided to retire from fishing, and they soon took up office work, happy to live a more calm and peaceful life. The fourth man, the man who prayed, continued on with lobstering, able to enjoy the open sea again, with a renewed faith and belief in the power of prayer, and in "the Big Daddy upstairs." He considered himself a living miracle, trusting that his life was saved and would continue to be saved even in the most drastic and horrific circumstances.

HONEY

Honey called me last week on a drizzly Tuesday night and asked me to meet her under the bridge at Riverside Park. She sounded very upset, practically frantic, and when I asked her to stop by my place instead, she refused saying it was too dangerous. That made no sense to me since going to the park at this late hour seemed more "dangerous" than getting together at my place. And Honey was such a nice girl I couldn't understand what was so life threatening, or so she said, that was causing her to behave like this.

Anyway I said yes, I'd meet her under the bridge at nine pm. That was half an hour from now, so I rushed out forgetting my umbrella, the mist and drizzle dampening my hair until water droplets dripped from my forehead. Luckily it was warm, so I didn't feel a chill in my wet attire. I got to the bridge and walked underneath, glad to be out of the elements. The soft sand was hard to walk in with my running shoes, but I didn't mind after hearing the gentle lapping of the water against the shore. It somehow felt relaxing to me. Honey wasn't there yet, so I sat down soaking up more of the peaceful vibe. I'd never been down to the river at night, and it didn't seem as dangerous as I had imagined after all. Not a soul was in sight, not that I could see anything very well, except for the light cast by the lamps that lit up the bike path nearby.

Five minutes later Honey arrived, the light from her flashlight bouncing and weaving, preceding her arrival. "Becca?" She called out.

"Yea, it's me," I replied standing up so she could see me better. "What's going on?"

She stepped in closer and I could see the mascara running down her face. I couldn't tell if it was because of the rain or if she had been crying. She grabbed me by the shoulders, then hugged me tight, so tight I had to catch my breath. "The reason why I had to meet you here in person is

… well … well you've been such a good friend to me that I didn't want to leave without saying goodbye."

"What do you mean? Leave?" Honey had been my closest friend for years, only lately I hadn't seen very much of her since she hooked up this new boyfriend. She moved in with him four months ago and I felt kind of like she dropped me for him. But I did understand since she hadn't had anyone in her life for such a long time. She was so happy, so I was happy for her too.

"I mean I have to leave town and … don't ask me why, I can't say." "But where will you go? I don't understand."

"I'm sorry Becca, but something's come up," tears welling in her eyes. "I just can't say right now…. Anyway, I wanted you to have this." Honey took out a jar of my favorite honey from her knapsack, the kind that was too expensive for me to buy. I'd only had it once before and it was phenomenal. She handed me the tall jar. "This is for you."

"Wow, thank you very much. I love this."

"I know you do. You always talked about how you put it on everything from your English muffins to your date nut bread and whatever." She started to cry, almost sob. "I have to go now. Take care of yourself." She hugged me again and took off running into the dark and rainy night.

I lay awake for several nights after, unable to sleep, wondering what had happened to her.

Then tonight on the news I heard that the police had caught the robbers in the Bells North Bank heist. They closed in on them in a shootout at a highway rest stop, the bank robbers taken into custody with minor wounds. I was shocked. It was my closest friend Honey and her boyfriend.

MEMORY LANE

Sarafina, intrigued when she passed by the street sign, hesitated a moment before doubling back and turning left, walking down the old paved road called *Memory Lane*. On each side of this little street were little brick homes, which once housed the copper miners from a time early in the last century; Sarafina had read that on a historical marker at the entrance to the small town where she planned to make just a brief stop to mail a package and then continue on her way, driving all the way to the east coast. But after mailing the package she decided to take a walk to stretch her legs and relax a little before she got back on the road for another several hours.

So here she was enjoying the fall afternoon walk through an unknown neighborhood. And so far it was very interesting with all things beautiful to look at and enjoy. Some of the brick homes were painted over in shades of green, blue and rust. Some were enclosed with small white picket fences and others had black wrought iron. Yards were decorated with colorful flowering pots of mums and marigolds; small statues of angels, children, and animals including ducks, deer, frogs and birds. There were flamingoes and sunflowers on sticks, carved out pumpkins and cobwebs too. One house had clucking chickens and roosters patrolling the yard. Several cats roamed freely down the street; one stopped to greet Sarifina before scampering up a small elm tree.

A big black poodle ran to a gate, startling Sarafina. She picked up her pace slightly until she came to the next house which made her stop dead in her tracks. The house looked exactly like her grandmother's, back on the East coast. This one was made of wood, just like her grandmother's. The windows and doors were all in the same place and everything was painted the exact same color as her grandmothers - sky blue, her favorite, with white trim.

Sarafina looked at the mailbox - Ethel Briggs was written in bright gold letters. It couldn't be.

That was her grandmother's name. Sarafina was stunned. This made no sense. Confused but curious, she opened the picket gate and walked up the cement-cracked path to the front door. She knocked. No one answered so she knocked again. Then she rang the bell. Footsteps; she heard footsteps coming down the hall. For a moment she considered running, leaving that very instant, but for some reason her feet stayed glued to the faded grey painted porch.

The door squeaked open, it's rusty hinges jarring her and comforting her at the same time. It sounded just like her grandmother's door. But this was crazy. Her grandmother had passed twenty-five years ago. Sarafina shut her eyes for a second and when she opened them, there was Ethel Briggs, her grandmother, standing right in front of her, in the flesh.

"Come in Sarafina," Ethel said, "I've been waiting for you." Sarafina's knees went weak and she almost toppled over if not for her grandmother reaching out to grab her arm. "I know you can't believe this, but it's true. Come in and I can explain everything to you, how all of this is happening … You know, I miss the times we've had with each other Sarafina. We were so close and I wanted to have another day together with you. So won't you come in and have tea with me. I have those oatmeal cinnamon raisin cookies you used to love too."

Sarafina was slowly regaining her composure. She had missed her grandmother terribly since she passed away and secretly held onto a wish that she could somehow be with her again. Today it seemed her dream was coming true. Sarafina took a step forward and walked through the door arm and arm with her grandmother where she would spend a most lovely, heartwarming and extraordinary afternoon.

PRIZE TENT

It was summer vacation and Francis had taken her three children to the fairgrounds that hot Saturday afternoon in Dragon Falls. Dad had extra work to catch up on at home so he didn't come along. Francis parked at the far end of the big dusty parking lot under an old eucalyptus tree and she and the children walked to the entrance and paid the admission fee. Once inside they saw lots of families milling about, children skipping with balloons, clowns riding on bicycles, a group of young men and woman seated in a ring playing ukuleles. There were smells from the food carts filling the air. Hot dogs were for sale, along with sausage and pepper sandwiches, tacos, roasted corn on the cob, popcorn and ice cream cones. There was so much to do but Jenny wanted to go on the rides first, so they bought the extra tickets and headed for the Octopus. Then they screamed in fun on the Scrambler and Round Up. Next was the Ferris Wheel and they enjoyed that too, although Belinda found out she was afraid of heights. Enough of the rides.

They walked over to the open air barn and looked at the animals: goats, pigs, rabbits and sheep. Some of them had blue, red or white ribbons tacked onto their pens, signaling first place, second and third. Next it was time for snacks. Belinda and Ben got Cotton Candy, and Jenny got a Carmel Candy Apple. They were sitting on the bench when Ben said, "Hey we never went in that big tent yet. I can see the sign from here … um … it says …Prize Tent."

"Let's go Mommy," Jenny said, "I want to go in the Prize Tent." They walked over and entered. It was crowded inside. It seemed to be the place where all the kids were gathering, hoping to go home with their arms filled with loot: colorful stuffed animals, plastic race cars….

Belinda ran over to the water guns and paid her ticket. She was a good shooter and her bell rang first. "We have a winner," the game attendant roared and Belinda pointed to the top shelf. She wanted the big yellow stuffed Tweety Bird. Then Ben and Jenny took their chances on the ball toss, trying to get it to land in the little holes. They both won a prize too - a toy truck for Ben and a teddy bear for Jenny.

It was getting very loud in the tent, with all the children squealing and shouting, the piercing laughter, hands clapping, bells ringing and piped in music playing over loud speakers. Francis said it was time for them to go home but the kids wanted to stay just a little longer. "No," Francis said, "It's time to go. Now!"

Ben complained again, but Francis was firm, "No, we are leaving now. You've had plenty of time for fun. Let's go."

The four started to make their way toward the exit when Francis heard the sound and saw the sizzling spark. The power went out, the lights went off. There was a shocking silence from everyone. Then the big tent above them gave way and began to tumble down onto the huge crowd below. Kids screamed and started running everywhere and soon everyone was covered with the heavy weight of white burlap. Francis and the kids were about ten feet from the exit by then so they were able to crawl out following a few people that were in front of them.

Firetrucks and ambulances were just turning into the parking lot as Francis and the kids ran back to their car. Ben, Belinda and Jenny were still crying. There were hundreds still trapped under the prize tent but it would turn out that no one was seriously hurt. Francis was grateful she told them to leave when she did, otherwise they wouldn't have been so close to the exit. She strapped on everyone's seatbelt exclaiming, "We will never go to an amusement park again!"

FRENCH DOORS

They said there was to be a big meteor shower that night. Christine awoke early that day, well before six am, and when she heard the birds begin to chirp she decided to get out of bed and make a fresh hot cup of caramel creme coffee. Scott was still sleeping on the comfy bed in their cozy rented casita and Christine was careful not to wake him. She sat on the brown leather recliner with her steaming cup and gazed out the French doors to the patio lined with royal blue deck chairs, a low wrought iron table and fire pit, which Scott had lit the evening before. The flames had burned bright after a couple of false starts, and when Scott ripped up a grocery bag for extra kindling, they enjoyed the heat and crackling fire for some time, until the smoke and flying ash burned their eyes.

Now, as her eyes drifted beyond the patio to the tall desert pine rising to meet the cloudless sky, Christine contemplated the coming event predicted for that evening. Would it be as spectacular as she imagined? Would the day pass quick enough to appease her growing excitement? Would she have a front row seat to one of the greatest shows on earth?

The stillness of the morning soon passed. Scott arose and they began their last day together on their vacation in this unique city, a temporary home-away-from-home which had thus far provided them with some quality time, free from the constant stress of everyday life. They drove the car downtown to the historic section and wandered into a small Italian restaurant where they shared an amazing calzone, filled with chicken, pesto, mozzarella, artichokes and red bell peppers. Meandering through the streets, they found a cool record store filled with vinyl albums from the 50's on up, along with tall book shelves lined with the latest fiction and biographies.

Scott discovered a rare LP from Sissy Spacek, and he was thrilled, having just finished her intriguing television series, *Night Sky*. The couple continued their explorations, enjoying the unique curio and clothing shops and art galleries, the churches and statues - and one in particular, a towering representation of *Our Lady of Guadalupe*. Late in the afternoon they stopped for coffee and peach croissants at a French bakery near the railroad yard. There was a fascinating installation on the property of a half buried flying saucer rising out of the ground. The owner's brother came out to join Christine and Scott in a pleasant conversation, relaying that the installation had just arrived the day before and they needed a huge crane and lots of cement positioned under the ground to get the artistic piece securely fastened. Christine found it very interesting that the bakery establishment was named *Sky Coffee*. Finally the two headed back to the casita just as the sun was setting.

Throughout that day, Christine had thoughts about that night's meteor shower, but she managed to direct them to the back of her mind. But now, back in their quiet space, shooting star visions came to the forefront, her excitement escalating.

Dinner and a glass or two of wine followed and then it was ten o'clock. Christine was getting sleepy. It was past her nine pm bedtime and she could barely keep her eyes open. Maybe she'd lie down, just for a few minutes, then get up and 'man the post,' keeping a sharp eye out the French doors for signs of shooting stars. She hoped for a huge display, but as she settled into the soft big bed, she immediately fell fast asleep. Scott soon followed her to the place of dreams.

Christine awoke with a start, and looked at the clock. It was 4:44. Oh no, she had missed it! She was sure of it! Bounding out of bed and racing to the French doors, she searched longingly

across the sky. She could see *The Big Dipper* and *Arcturus* directly overhead. But meteors and shooting stars - there was nothing. She waited for a while as a monstrous wave of disappointment overcame her. All this build-up - for zilch. Christine sighed a heavy sigh and tears began to cloud her eyes.

Suddenly ... a flash of light. A shooting star!... No, it didn't shoot; it slowed down ... and stopped ... it hovered, balancing in space, right in front of her. Christine was stunned. Could it really be ... a UFO?

The light flickered, blinked on, then off; a beam shot out and a stream of light rapidly came rushing toward her. Christine froze in fear, unable to move as the light entered her chest. It felt like a small grade electric shock but left her unharmed. As the energy spread throughout her body, a massive wave of calm entered every cell of her being. Christine breathed deep, feeling more relaxed than she ever had before, all the tenseness in her shoulders and neck completely vanishing, leaving her mind clear and spirit free. She raised a hand as if to say thank you ... just as the ship turned and sped off, disappearing far into the night.

STICKS

The sticks looked like they were set for a campfire. The hikers had trekked five miles through the wilderness when they came upon those sticks. Mike stopped short and Ruth nearly ran into him. "Look, someone must be nearby." Mike stepped aside for Ruth to observe not just the neatly arranged sticks, but also two bottles of tea, an old red blanket and a jackknife beside it.

"What'll we do?" Ruth nervously hissed. "Who knows what kind of people are out here. And we're far away from getting any help. It could be days before anyone found us."

"Let's keep going. I'm sure we'll be fine." Mike wanted to make it to the top of the peak by sunset, where they would set up camp, enjoy supper by campfire, and gaze at the stars overhead.

"Alright," Ruth responded reluctantly, "but I hope we don't run into anyone." It was off season and Ruth was looking forward to a private Californian retreat in the mountains. They set off again, moving beyond the sticks and had gone four hundred yards when Mike heard singing.

"Listen." He held up a hand. They stood motionless, taking in the sweet melody, silver-toned and enchanting, like the prettiest of birds. The voice sounded young too, perhaps coming from a girl in her late teens. They lost all fear, and curious to see who this girl was, they stepped past the trees and heavy brush blocking their view. The woods opened to a small field of green grasses swaying in the breeze. And there in the middle was the girl also swaying ... and spinning and singing. She had long flowing blond hair, delicate features, and wore faded blue jeans and a light blue blouse. As she spun around again, she caught a glimpse of Mike and Ruth and froze.

"You scared me. I didn't know anyone was here," she practically whispered. Then her voice took on the tough tone of someone intent on protecting themself. "Don't come any closer! My boyfriend is a

130

cop. And he's just beyond those trees." She glared and pointed to the trees ahead.

"Don't worry. We won't hurt you. We heard singing and wanted to see who it was," Mark said. "By the way, you have a beautiful voice."

"Thanks," the girl replied. "Now, I have to get going." She picked up her duffle bag and made moves to go, though it appeared she didn't know which direction to take.

"We saw your campfire sticks back there," Ruth blurted.

"Yes, my boyfriend and I were … were … oh, forget it. I don't have a boy friend. I just said that … I was scared."

"That's ok," Ruth nodded sympathetically. "But you have me thinking …" and she looked at Mark who nodded in agreement, knowing what Ruth was about to say. "You, young lady, have one of the most outstanding voices I've heard in a long time. Would you mind singing another song for me? How about *Five Hundred Miles*, if you know it." Ruth wanted to make sure this potential brilliance wasn't just some fluke.

"Yes, I know that one. My Mom taught me that when I was five." And she began a phenomenal rendition of the Peter, Paul and Mary hit. When she finished, everyone was quiet.

Ruth smiled, "When I'm not hiking, I search for new talent. I run an agency where we place music and songs in television and film. I'd like you to come to my office to record some tracks for a new TV series I'm working on. And, I have some more projects for you to do after that."

The girl was overwhelmed. Singing in the biz, becoming a star, had been her desire since she was twelve and heard Vanessa Hudgens sing in *High School Musical*. Now here she was being discovered, in almost deserted woods in the middle of nowhere.

131

THE RECLUSE

They left the recluse standing in the moonlight by the barbed wire coiled gate. Harry was an old friend of Tom and Wilma's, and very good friend at one time. They hung around with him all through high school. Harry had always been the life of the party back then, surrounded by a big group of friends who admired everything about him: his confident personality, his sense of humor, his charming good looks. And Harry had been the best man at Tom and Wilma's wedding when they married that summer after graduation, giving the newlyweds a really funny toast.

But something changed in Harry soon after that. He kept to himself more and more, moved into an apartment alone at the far side of town and took a job as a late night security guard at the plastics plant down by the river. No one saw him around town anymore and he wouldn't return Tom and Wilma's phone calls, so after a while they gave up calling him.

It had been two years, and today was Harry's birthday. Wilma and Tom came home from work and during supper they started to reminisce about all the good times they'd had together. "Remember that night when Harry drove donuts around the supermarket parking lot in his beat- up green chevy pickup?" Tom laughed.

"Yea, that was fun. I was getting so dizzy too…. And remember when Harry dressed up as a lady vampire that Halloween when we were seniors. He looked so cute," Wilma added.

"That was a riot…. Hey since it's his birthday today why don't we go down to the plant and surprise him with a birthday cake. He usually works at night. I bet he'd get a kick out of that."

"That sounds like a great idea. I do have a good recipe for a chocolate one. I can whip it up in no time."

"Cool," said Tom, "I'll clear the dishes and help you with it."

About an hour and a half later, they packed the vanilla-frosted chocolate cake in a box along with some candles and headed down to the plastics plant. Outside the gate they lit all twenty candles on the cake and started to sing Happy Birthday. They didn't see Harry at first, but they knew with the noise they were making that he would be coming by. A second later a flashlight shone in their faces.

"Happy birthday, Harry!" they yelled. "Who's that? Who's that?"

"It's us Harry, Tom and Wilma, your friends from high school," Tom said. "What?"

"Tom and Wilma." "What? What?"

"Tom and Wilma, from high school Harry," Wilma repeated. "What?" Harry said again, totally ignoring the lit up birthday cake. "We brought you a birthday cake. Happy Birthday!"

"What? What?" He wasn't getting what they were saying and kept repeating *what,* like he couldn't hear them. Tom and Wilma were beginning to think he had gone deaf. They weren't sure what to do. They tried one more time to break through to him. He still said, "What? What?"

Tom and Wilma blew out the candles, picked up the cake and headed for the car, leaving Harry standing by the moon lit gate. Harry grinned and laughed a hollow laugh, glad they were fooled, glad to be rid of them.

RIPPLING WAVES

Strange waves rippled around the earth. This was the headline posted on Everett McKenzie's twitter and instagram page. Everett, a scuba diver with a blue shark tattoo on one calf and a red sting ray on the other, was a man with drive and purpose. He wanted to be famous - the first one, and the oldest one to dive the deepest in the Atlantic Ocean. He wished to have his name and accomplishment listed in the Guinness Book of World Records. Although his health had started to decline, he figured he could make one more dive, achieve his goal and die a happy man.

On an afternoon in late June, Everett donned his scuba gear and dove off the rented boat into the deepest part of the ocean. Since he had been a mathematician all his life, he had plenty of time and opportunity to make the correct calculations on exactly where to dive. Sinking down into the depths, he began his adventure with his underwater camera, shooting several interesting shots of the sea creatures in their natural habitat: playful florescent yellow and orange fish, rusty- colored octopus' retreating down to their rock dens, schools of yellow fin tuna eyeing him as they swam past, along with the occasional Southern stingray, which luckily, they all turned and swam away when they saw the diver. He hoped to avoid barracudas though, and so far he was lucky, he hadn't seen any.

Everett swam down deeper, careful to check his pressure gauge for any potential warning signs. All appeared well so he dropped down even deeper. He could see the bottom two hundred yards away…. Suddenly Everett's scuba mask shattered. There was a tiny, unnoticeable hairline crack which occurred that morning when a boat attendant, assisting Everett with loading up, accidentally dropped the mask. Now, water came rushing in and Everett, unable to stay down any longer, rose to the surface defeated. This was his last chance to make the world's record; he would be too old, not healthy enough to make the dive again.

Sitting aboard the vessel, chin in his hands and mourning his loss, Everett noticed a rippling wave, followed by several more, that came rushing toward him from the starboard side. When the waves came within ten yards of the boat, they rose high up into the air above Everett's head. They seemed to float there, gently suspended. Everett was stunned, and for a moment he was unable to move. Then he bolted into action, scrambling to find his state-of-the-art seismic meter, suitable for recording an event such as this. He trained the meter on the waves and just as he did so, the waves took off and headed west. They moved slow at first, then picked up speed and were soon out of sight. However the seismic meter kept track of them, documenting a full passage around the earth.

Not sure why this was happening, Everett decided to report it to the local television news station, and to see if anyone else had made a similar claim. He found there were no other reports of rippling wave sightings. In addition, the people at the television station laughed at him. They didn't believe him or take him seriously, thinking he was just one more crazy in today's mixed up world. They got security to escort him out of the building. So Everett went home and posted the news on his Twitter and Instagram page. It went viral. Soon UFO enthusiasts and other conspiracy theorists appeared outside his house, parking themselves in his yard and on his doorstep. Everett couldn't even leave the house without being stopped by one or the other, each badgering him to tell them more…. Everett got his wish. He was famous alright, though not nearly in the way he planned or expected it.

YELLOW SUNFLOWERS

Alice glared at the empty plate on the kitchen table in front of her, decorated with bright yellow sunflowers. It's cheeriness didn't suit her mood, so she grabbed an extra dark chocolate bar from the refrigerator and began to nibble on that. Maybe washing down the fried ham and egg breakfast sandwich that Spencer had made with a little dark chocolate would help. Spencer was upstairs now, packing his suitcase, and in another hour he would be on his way … again … to another book signing tour for his latest novel in the popular who-done-it mystery series, *The Stephanopolis Cases.* The last time he was away it was for two months, but this time he would be gone for four months, and that was just too long for Alice; she *was not* happy. Alice had asked if she could go with him, but Spencer said no. She would only be bored or lonely with nothing to do since he would be busy the whole time. Alice didn't see it that way. She'd rather be anywhere with him than stuck at home trapped behind these four walls. And the small planes flying over their house day after day were driving her nuts. The couple didn't know it before they moved to this beautiful old home that they were directly under the flight path of planes taking off from the small airport three miles away. So there was a constant barrage of buzzing and roaring from pilots keeping up their license requirements and students learning to fly. And Spencer wouldn't move. He was happy living in this house. Well, he wasn't stuck there all the time, like Alice.

Alice got up to pack Spencer a cooler with a few turkey and muenster sandwiches and some carrot sticks, a couple little bags of potato chips, some water bottles and ice tea. She wandered the kitchen and stopped by the window, looking out at the mountain in the distance. She heard the shower water running upstairs and knew Spencer was in the bathroom. That's when she hatched the idea. It was brilliant. A really excellent one she thought - and now to execute it. She ran upstairs and told Spencer that she just got a phone call from her brother and that he needed her help, something

136

he couldn't talk about over the phone but she must go over to see him right away. "Okay," Spencer said as she kissed his cheek, his face wet from the shower water. "I'll see you when I get back."

"Right, I'll see you," Alice said as Spencer stepped back under the shower. She ran to the guest room and pulled a spare suitcase from the closet. Then she went to the bedroom and quickly threw in some clothes: a couple pairs of blue jeans, a pair of dress pants, a few colored blouses, a sweater and light jacket, underwear and some shoes, including her favorite turquoise pumps. She was very careful not to make any noise since Spencer was right next door. She could tell he was just about to finish his shower because he had stopped singing. Alice tiptoed downstairs and added a few snacks to her baggage: a box of crackers, a couple apples, more chocolate bars, a can of peanuts and some water. Then she bolted out the door heading straight for Spencer's sedan. She popped the trunk and hopped inside, closing it with the red, blue and white polyester rope she hooked in a loop. Now all she had to do was wait. Spencer would be at least seven hours out of town before she would bang on the trunk door, letting him know she was there - too late for him to turn back and take her home.

Alice laughed quietly as Spencer closed and locked the front door to the house. He put his suitcase in the backseat and started the car. Alice pulled out a chocolate bar and unwrapped it. She took a big bite, feeling just as cheerful and bright-eyed as those big yellow sunflowers on her breakfast plate.

ANGEL WINGS

She wore angel wings on her back - sparkling glitter wings adhered to a long black shirt.

Today was the first day Roxanne wore that shirt, and because she was so unusually tall - towering over the rest of the staff, male and female - combined with her golden blond curls and thin frame, she made for a very striking appearance. The agency's Christmas party was being held that afternoon and work was cut short when preparations began in the conference room.

Barbara just finished the table arrangements and began carving the roast turkey when Roxanne entered the room. Dorothy was reheating mashed potatoes in the microwave. "What did you bring to the party?" Barbara asked smugly. Everyone in the office considered Roxanne an oddball and was extremely jealous that she was recently promoted to the coveted executive manager position ahead of themselves. They all wanted to bring home the better paycheck that went along with the advance in status and rank amidst their peers. To say that competition was high between workers was an understatement.

"I brought those red and green sparkle Christmas butter cookies," replied Roxanne.

Barbara snickered and rolled her eyes at Dorothy. Dorothy pouted her lips. Bruce walked in with his green bean casserole and placed it on the banquet table covered with a paper tablecloth decorated with printed Christmas trees, ornaments and bells, fireplaces and stockings. He grimaced when he saw Roxanne and made himself busy adjusting the centerpiece of pine and holly. Then he maneuvered the punch bowl and the egg nog into place, not saying a word to anyone. More people drifted in, got a drink and sat at the several small tables arranged along the sides of the room. Someone turned on the CD player and Christmas songs drifted softly in the background. Everyone looked a bit glum for Christmas, talking amongst themselves, casting disparaging looks in Roxanne's direction. No one could believe that the *Big Boss* gave her the job. She had only been with the company three months and the rest of them had been there years. What did Roxanne have that they didn't? They shook their heads, shrugged their shoulders, scoffed at her advancement.

Roxanne stood in the corner taking it all in. She could hear everything they were saying, see their demeaning looks. She waited another five minutes until everyone in the office had arrived. Everyone except the *Big Boss*. Then she walked to the center of the room, raised her right hand and whistled with her left. All quieted down and looked at her. Roxanne began to hum and then to sing, "Hark the herald angels sing ..." No one said a word, no one joined in.

But then the most amazing thing happened. The angel wings on the back of Roxanne's shirt suddenly began to glow bright, the light from them emanating a stream of circular rays that cut through to every corner of the room, casting a shine on all the people there. The employees eyes widened and then there was a collective gasp as Roxanne herself took on a luminescent appearance, her whole body was a vibrant white glistening light. She slowly turned around looking into the eyes of all her co-workers. "Do you all know why you are here?" she asked with complete calmness echoing in her voice.... These were the only words she spoke before she smiled, and in a burst of shimmering exhilarating light Roxanne was gone, disappearing into a flash of glimmering mist that twinkled and vanished right before everyone's eyes.

Made in the USA
Middletown, DE
07 November 2024

63660456R00086